Dear Brio Girl,

What do guys really look for in a girl? How do the clothes you wear affect them? How do they talk about girls when there's no one around but guys? Here's your chance to find out—straight from a guy!

Go ahead. Make the plunge. Get inside Tyler's head and heart and discover how a guy thinks and feels. You'll never forget what you'll learn in the next few pages!

Your Friend,

Susie Shellenberger, BRIO
Editor
www.briomag.com

Brio Girls

Stuck in the Sky
by Lissa Halls Johnson

Fast Forward to Normal
by Jane Vogel

Opportunity Knocks Twice
by Lissa Halls Johnson

Double Exposure
by Kathy Wierenga

brio girls

REAL Faith MEETS REAL Life

Jacie Hannah Solana Becca

Opportunity knocks Twice

Created by
LISSA HALLS JOHNSON

BETHANYHOUSE
MINNEAPOLIS, MINNESOTA

Focus on the Family books are available at special quantity discounts when purchased in bulk by corporations, organizations, churches, or groups. Special imprints, messages, and excerpts can be produced to meet your needs. For more information, contact: Resource Sales Group, Focus on the Family, 8605 Explorer Drive, Colorado Springs, CO 80920; phone (800) 932-9123.

A Focus on the Family book.
Published by Bethany House Publishers
A Ministry of Bethany Fellowship International
11400 Hampshire Avenue South
Bloomington, Minnesota 55438
www.bethanyhouse.com

Printed in the United States of America by
Bethany Press International, Bloomington, Minnesota 55438

Library of Congress Cataloging-in-Publication Data

Johnson, Lissa Halls, 1955-
   Opportunity knocks twice / created by Lissa Halls Johnson.
      p. cm. — (Brio girls)
Summary: When his old girlfriend moves back to town, Tyler worries that dating her again will interfere with his friendships, especially with the beautiful Hannah, and draw him away from God.
    ISBN 1-56179-953-X
    [1. Interpersonal relations—Fiction. 2. Dating (Social customs)—Fiction. 3. Christian life—Fiction.] I. Title. II. Series.
    PZ7.J63253 Op   2002
[Fic]—dc21
                                                 2001006280

LISSA HALLS JOHNSON is on staff at Focus on the Family where she writes some books, edits others and torments her co-workers with outrageous questions, flying toys, and generally being a nuisance. When she's not held captive by her gray cubicle, she's hanging out at the foot of the mountains she adores, usually hiking in the Garden of the Gods with her dog, Ginger. Previously a member of the ADVENTURES IN ODYSSEY creative team, she's completely surprised that she's the author of fifteen novels for teens and the young reader.

c h a p t e r

Mom's going to kill me, Tyler thought, pushing the gas pedal even further down as his old Escort screeched around a corner.

"Whoa!" Richard said, grabbing the armrest. "Hey, didn't you ever take Driver's Ed?"

"Driver's what?" Tyler said.

"Where's a cop when you need one?" Richard grumbled.

"What time is it?" Tyler asked.

"You've got a watch."

"You want me to take my eyes off the road to—"

"One-fifteen! One-fifteen!" Richard shouted. "Hey, this is a 45 zone. What're you doin'—80?"

Tyler glanced at the speedometer; it read 50. "Ninety," he said. "Did I mention my mom is going to kill me?"

"She better be quick, then, or else some telephone pole is gonna save her the trouble."

Tyler shook his head, disgusted at himself. "You know the last thing she told me before I left for basketball fitness training this morning?"

"Sign your will? Check the brakes? Get airbags installed in that old death trap you drive? Don't kill Richard?"

" 'Don't be late,' she said. 'The photo shoot is set for one o'clock, and if you're late everyone will have to wait for you. Try to be early.' That's what she said. And now look. After workout, I stood around talking with you guys until—"

"Tyler, you think she's going to feel better knowing that, even though you were already 15 minutes late, you died and killed your best friend rushing to get there—"

"You my best friend, Richard?" Tyler asked, cutting quickly to the left to pull around an old Buick about the size of a supermarket, driven by a little 100-year-old man in a fedora, stretching his neck to peer over the dashboard.

"If you'll slow down to within 20 miles of the speed limit, I'll be your best friend for the rest of our lives, which might be quite a while for me if I never ride with you again."

"Oh yeah? Then why won't you put a band together with me? I need a drummer." Tyler pushed the pedal harder; the car roared louder.

"Oh, please, man, anything but that. I'll let you have my Beatles CD collection. I'll do your homework for you. I'll let you go out with my girlfriend. I'll—"

"Why would I want you to do my homework, Richard? You have a C-plus average. And you don't have a girlfriend."

"I'll get one so you can go out with her. Okay, you're right about the homework. Hey, why don't you do *my* homework, as long as we're going to be best friends? Why don't—" Richard stopped talking when Tyler hit the brakes, throwing them both against their seat belts. "What . . ."

"We're here. Probably not a good idea to speed into the Focus on the Family parking lot on the way to a photo shoot and run over somebody."

"Oh, no, of course not," Richard said as Tyler pulled sedately into the parking lot, a model of courteous, defensive driving. "Run over as many nuns and baby carriages as you possibly can out on the street, but—"

"There they are," Tyler said, spotting his group standing on the grass on the unseasonably warm afternoon. "Be on your best behavior."

"Can I puke in the bushes first? I feel the need."

"Hold it. Puke later." Tyler pulled into an empty place not far from where the group of girls stood—five of them, apparently waiting for his mom to come out and get them. He honked, waved, smiled, and got out of the car.

Richard followed him across the grass. "Do any of these girls know how you drive?" he said under his breath.

"Not the ones who are still living."

"Ah."

As he and Richard approached the girls, Becca raised an eyebrow at Tyler, glanced at her watch, and looked back at him pointedly. Tyler smiled. He'd known she'd be ticked, and Solana, too. But it was really his mom he felt worst about letting down. This was her job, after all.

Jacie looked up at him, smiled sweetly, and said, "Gosh, boys, you're too late. Sorry. We just finished." She tilted her head and gave a look Tyler couldn't quite read. She glanced toward the other girls and back to Tyler.

"Good, now we can go home," Richard said. "Jacie, can I ride back with you?"

Jacie, Becca, and Solana were Tyler's oldest and closest friends, going all the way back to fourth grade. He couldn't remember ever *not* knowing them. He had plenty of guy friends, like Richard, but there really was no one he knew as well—and who knew him as well—as the "Brio girls," as they called themselves. Except maybe his sister, Tyra, who was three years younger.

But it was the tall, blonde girl who was new to the group, Hannah Connor, whom Tyler had really been looking forward to seeing. She was talking excitedly to a shorter, dark-haired girl who had her back to him. Tyler wasn't sure who the shorter girl was; probably the daughter of somebody who worked with Tyler's mom. There was something familiar about her figure—which was *awfully* good—or her way of standing—which was *awfully* alluring. Maybe she'd been to one of these shoots before, or maybe he had met her at a Focus Christmas party.

Tyler's mother was on the staff of *Brio* magazine, published by Focus on the Family. For the past few years, she had used Tyler, Becca, Jacie, and Solana (all three of the girls were avid readers of *Brio* and thought Tyler's mom had about the coolest job in the world) as models for the magazine. This shoot, on the Saturday after Thanksgiving, was the second time they'd been called up this school year—so, since this was Hannah's first year at the school, it was only the second time she'd been involved. Maybe that would account for her excitement.

But what, Tyler wondered, accounted for the strange looks he was getting from Jacie, Becca, and Solana? Each of the three was studying him carefully, as if he'd done something wrong. Or was about to. And was that sympathy in Jacie's eyes?

"Hey," he said. "I'm sorry I'm late. Where's Mom?"

"Inside trying to call you," Solana said, her eyes continually looking toward the dark-haired mystery girl, as if trying to get him to do something.

"What? Do you want me to—"

"Tyler!" Hannah said, as if she were noticing him for the first time, even though he'd seen her cut her eyes at him twice while she was talking to the other girl, who still faced away from him. "I have somebody I want you to meet. Or maybe you already know her. She used to live here, then she moved away, and now she's back. So I thought maybe . . ."

Hannah kept talking, but Tyler didn't hear a word of it. Because the dark-haired girl turned around. And Tyler knew immediately what had seemed familiar about her. You get that way about somebody you were in love with for a year.

"Anyway," Hannah continued, "I want you to meet Jessica Abbott. Jessica, this is—"

"Hello, Tyler," Jessica said, in that voice she had, smiling that little smile she used only for him. Or used to.

And she stepped close, put her soft arms around his neck, kissed his cheek, nestled her head against his neck sweetly for a second— what a rush of memory!—then stepped away before it became obvious that Tyler hadn't moved a muscle.

"Uh . . ." Tyler said. And that's all he could manage. An awkward silence descended upon the whole group.

Some stupid bird tweeted somewhere.

Other than the stupid bird, Tyler was aware only of Jessica's smile, her face, her eyes that he had looked into so closely so often and had last seen—when?—almost exactly a year ago.

"What's this?" Becca said. "The great Tyler Jennings speechless?"

"Uh . . ." he said again, and looked at the three Brio girls.

"You already said that," Solana pointed out.

Come on, Tyler, he thought. *Say something, you idiot.*

"Say something, you idiot," Richard hissed in his ear. Then, to Jessica, Richard said, "Hey, Jessica, nice to see you. So, you back for good or what? Because we've been looking for a way to shut Tyler up, and if you're going to stick around, maybe—*oof!*" This last was spoken with Tyler's left elbow firmly planted just below the ribs on Richard's right side.

With a confused glance at Jacie, Becca, and Solana, Tyler turned to Jessica and said, "Yeah, I guess I'm surprised, is all. I mean . . . you look great. Wow. I mean—what a surprise!"

"I think he said that already, too, didn't he?" Solana said.

"Yes, I believe he did—you mean about being surprised?" Becca said.

"Yeah, that part."

"Becca, Solana," Tyler said sweetly, "I think it's feeding time, and they're beginning to throw the mackerel into the water. Better hurry back to the tank. So, Jessica—wow. When did you arrive?"

Still smiling, she said, "Just Wednesday night. It was all pretty quick. My dad's company wanted him to return here, and so—well, I really didn't know anything about it till four days ago, and now here I am. I'm not even registered for school yet! Sorry I didn't call or anything. The weirdest thing is Hannah's dad and my dad work together. We just met at Thanksgiving dinner." Jessica smiled at Hannah, who looked completely at a loss—and she was rather lovely at a loss, Tyler decided, the same as she was any other way. "She invited me to come to the shoot, so . . ."

"So," Hannah said. "I guess you two did know each other, then?"

"That right, Tyler?" Becca asked. "You knew each other?"

"Oh, Becca, stop it," Jessica laughed, that tinkling-bell laugh she had. "You're teasing him. Be nice." She turned toward Hannah. "Tyler and I went out for a while. Until I moved."

"Oh," Hannah said quietly.

Went out for a while? Is that how Jessica thought of it? Or was she just being cautious until she scoped out the situation? Because what they'd had definitely qualified for a more serious description than "went out for a while."

Tyler looked into Hannah's eyes and tried to read what he saw there. Was it disappointment? Concern? Jealousy? It was something. He couldn't tell what. But there was something there. And with a shock, Tyler realized that suddenly he didn't know what he wanted her to be feeling. Not anymore.

Because in the past two minutes, everything had changed.

And Tyler had no idea what that change meant.

● ● ●

"We'll talk tonight about you being late," Tyler's mom whispered as the two of them trailed the rest of the group moving down the long hallway to the studio where they would shoot today. "For now—" She motioned discreetly toward Jessica. "How long have you known about this?"

"Honest, Mom," Tyler whispered, "I had no idea she was even moving back here, much less that she was going to show up today."

"Well, I'll have to talk to Hannah about that. I like to choose the models, thank you very much."

Tyler braced himself for what he suspected was coming next. He knew his mom didn't really like Jessica. But she walked along quietly until Alicia, the photographer's assistant, came running up, smiled at Tyler, and then pulled his mom away to check on something.

Tyler looked for the girls, but they had disappeared, so he ducked into the men's restroom and found Richard there, standing in front of the mirror.

"Well, that was an unexpected development," Richard said, looking at his face from first one angle, then another. His close-cropped hair didn't need much attention. "But what I can't figure out is—"

"Don't even start," Tyler warned. "I need time to think." But where to begin? On the one hand, there was Hannah—breathtakingly beautiful, sweet and kind, but committed to the concept of "courtship" as opposed to dating. Meaning that Tyler, or any other guy, wouldn't be spending any "romantic" time with Hannah until he was serious about the possibility of *marrying* her. *Marriage!* As in forever. And even then, only under the close supervision of her parents. Still, Tyler had been subtly communicating to her since he'd met her at the beginning of the school year that he was interested in her. Not that he'd gotten anywhere. She seemed far more interested in being a strong spiritual influence on everybody she met than in the flash and buzz of romance. She hadn't even seemed flattered at his advances, if he was going to be honest with himself, although he was sure he detected some attraction there. Or maybe just hoped he did.

Richard cleared his throat. "I thought you had a thing for—"

"Hush." Then on the other hand there was the lovely Jessica. As shocked and happy as Tyler was to see her, she was now a problem. How could Tyler show her the affection he would like to without blowing his chances—if he had any—with Hannah? And if he ignored Jessica today, would she be hurt and not want to date him?

Tyler looked at himself in the mirror. He could almost imagine a little bubble over his head on one side with Hannah in it, another bubble on the other side with Jessica. Caught in the middle. Which would he choose?

He shook his head a little to see if his long, sun-bleached hair would fall into place. It usually did. Today, though, maybe because of his basketball workout that morning, it seemed stiff. Great.

They caught up with the girls out in the hallway and strolled toward the studio. Tyler wasn't even sure where to walk. Next to Jessica? But what would that say to Hannah—or for that matter, to the other girls, who were sure to be watching developments between Tyler and Jessica with great interest? In fact, he knew he would hear all about it the next time the three girls had him to themselves.

Jessica turned and gave him an amused smile over her shoulder. He knew exactly what that smile, that raised eyebrow, meant. She was saying, "This situation is so silly! But we'll get together soon and straighten it out, just the two of us."

They smelled it before they'd even opened the door to the studio. "Pizza!" Richard shouted.

"Shhh!" Becca said, finger to her lips and her brows knit together. "People are working."

"Working?" Tyler asked. "It's a Saturday."

"Besides, how can anybody work with the aroma of fresh pepperoni wafting through the halls?" the unrepentant and still-too-loud Richard asked, pushing the studio door open.

The studio was set up like a restaurant or cafeteria, and there were four large pizzas still in steaming, flat boxes on a round table, surrounded by chairs. A bucket of ice on the table held cans of several varieties of soda.

Tyler and Richard nodded. "Yes, there are times when it pays to have a mother who works for a magazine," Richard said. "Congratulations, Ty."

The photographer—his name was Jack, a young black guy who Tyler thought was pretty cool—stepped up on his ladder so he would be higher than everybody else. Which made sense, considering that he was about six inches shorter than Tyler. "Hey, everybody," Jack said.

"Hey," they all replied in unison.

"You already smelled the pizza, so I'll keep this short. All you have to do is dig in. Alicia will show you where to sit, and we'll move you around a little bit as I shoot, too. These first shots are just your basic kids-at-a-pizza-party, so no special instructions—except Tyler, don't pick your nose, and Hannah, no dancing on the tables."

"He forgot to tell me to chew with my mouth closed," Richard said as he plopped into the seat Alicia steered him toward. "Big mistake." He pulled a huge slice of double-cheese pizza onto a Styrofoam plate, strings of hot cheese trailing behind.

Tyler breathed a silent prayer of thanks that Alicia was assigning the seats, because that at least saved him the embarrassment of deciding who he was going to sit by. She put him right between Jacie and Hannah, as it turned out, right across from Jessica. Not bad, he decided. Definitely could have been worse.

As Tyler and the rest chowed down, Jack shouted out instructions: "Okay, somebody's telling a hilarious joke—everybody laugh!"

And a couple of minutes later: "Your football team just lost the championship game. Even the pizza can't make you feel better."

"Are you kidding?" Richard said. "If our team even got *into* the championship game, we wouldn't care if they lost by 60 points, the quarterback broke his leg, and the center played the whole game with a big split down the back of his pants—we'd still celebrate! It would be a school first!"

"Okay, this time we got a clique going here, and somebody's left out—Solana, you're the odd woman out. Look lonely and rejected. The rest of you are having a great time and don't even realize she's there."

"How hard will that be?" Solana asked. "They don't know I'm here half the time anyway."

After an hour, during which Jack shot several rolls of film, he stepped down off the ladder, wiped his forehead with a rag, and said, "Okay, take five."

"Well, thanks," Richard said, "but I'll be lucky if I can eat even *four* more."

"Tyler, could I see you a minute?" his mom asked.

Tyler hopped up and followed her. She went back to her office, and he plopped into a chair. "What?" he asked.

She grabbed some papers off her desk, turned to leave, and winked at him. "Nothing. You just looked like you could use some rescuing."

Tyler smiled. "Bless you, Mom. Did I ever tell you you're the best mom in the whole world?"

She nodded. "Yes. Pretty much every time I save your rear end." She blew him a kiss and left.

● ● ●

The pizza had been cleared from the tables when they got back, but the soda bucket had been refreshed—and, Tyler noticed happily, they had added some Dr Pepper this time. And—yes!—a couple of plates of Mrs. Fields's chocolate chip cookies. He opened a can of Dr Pepper and took a swig. *Ahhh.*

"Okay, the deal this time is," Jack explained, "we've got one couple madly in love. The two of you are so wrapped up in each other that you're shutting everybody else out."

Tyler glanced first at Hannah, then at Jessica.

"Everything—eye contact, body language, where you're sitting, everything—communicates that the two of you exist in your own little world. Some of the others notice it and feel excluded; others are just going on with their own conversations." He pointed to two chairs that Alicia was positioning close together. "Okay, Tyler, grab a partner, and you two lovebirds sit there."

Tyler choked on his Dr Pepper, coughed, wiped the moisture from his lips. Becca laughed out loud. "Me?" he said when he could speak.

"Yeah. Just choose whichever of these young ladies you'd like to spend the rest of your life with—" Obviously, Jack thought this was a very funny line. He had no idea. "—and cuddle up in those two chairs." Jack waited a moment, smiling, then said, "Hey, come on, you're all friends here. It's no big deal, right?"

"No," Tyler said. "I mean, *yeah*, it *is* a big deal. You give me the five most beautiful girls in Colorado and tell me I have to pick just *one?* That's cruel, man." *Think fast, Tyler. No dead air—everyone's waiting.* "It's an embarrassment of riches, Jack. Are you sure I can't have all five? I'd be the envy of every guy in school. Come on. Please?" *Oh, man—I'll never get out of this alive. If I choose Jessica, then—*

"Well, Tyler," Solana said. "Which of us lovely young ladies will it be?"

Suddenly Jacie laughed and began to jump up and down, her hand raised. "Me! Me! Pick me, Tyler!"

And immediately, Becca and Solana took her cue and began to jump up themselves, waving their arms for his attention. "Me, Tyler! Don't pick her! Pick me!"

"You see how it is, Jack?" Tyler said. "This is my life. Everybody wants me, but not everyone can have me. Well, today . . ." He looked around the group. "I choose . . ." He raised a hand slowly, waited—then touched Jacie's outstretched hand. "Jacie the Kind, Jacie the Wise . . . Jacie the Lucky."

She linked arms with him, leaned her head back against his shoulder, and gazed longingly up at him, batting her eyelashes. "Oh, Tyler. If I'd only known sooner how you felt. All this wasted time."

"Okay, Jacie it is," Jack said, climbing onto his ladder again, cameras and lenses dangling from his neck. "What a perfect couple. To your places, everyone. Lovebirds coo; the rest of you grab a cookie and a Coke and react."

Tyler put his hand over Jacie's and squeezed, looking into her eyes with gratitude. She smiled back a clear message: *You owe me.*

● ● ●

"I don't get it," Tyler said, driving home after the shoot had ended. "What was the deal with Becca and Solana? I was in serious trouble there, and they thought it was funny!"

Richard chuckled. "It *was* funny, man! I mean, I'm sorry, but there you were, the chick you've been chasing since September on one hand, Miss Nordic Queen, Barbie the Hutt, and on the other, the old flame, Miss Megabucks America. And you're standing in the middle, both of them waiting to see what you're going to do, and you're going, 'Duh—' "

"I didn't say, 'Duh,' " Tyler objected.

"I don't care if you *said* it or not—you *said* it, you know what I mean? Anyway, it was almost what you'd expect to see in some stupid movie or TV show. Which one will he choose? Whose heart will he break? Will Megabucks and Barbie slug it out, pulling hair and breaking bra straps to see who gets the handsome surf rat—*hey!*" He reached desperately to save his milk shake from Tyler. Drops flew in all directions as the top pulled loose.

"I'm not wasting a good milk shake on an idiot like you, pal," Tyler said. "Let loose. Gimme."

"This is mine!" Richard objected. "You bought it for me!"

"I want it now."

"You *had* one! You already finished it!"

"I don't want it to drink. I want it to pour over your head."

With a mighty heave, Richard managed to wrest the milk shake from Tyler's grasp and slumped against the far door. He slurped in triumph.

"What kind of friend are you, anyway?" Tyler asked. "You could have done something to help, instead of making things worse."

"I did help," Richard said, and he sounded serious for a change. "As usual, I made a spectacle of myself. Think about it. Every time I opened my mouth, attention shifted away from you for a minute, giving you an opportunity to make like Bugs Bunny and dig a burrow to China, leaving just a little molehill of dirt where an embarrassed moron used to be."

"Okay, pardner," Tyler said, "in gratitude for the great effort you made to bail me out today, even though it didn't work, I'm going to offer you a once-in-a-lifetime opportunity."

Richard snorted. "Here it comes. No, I'm fine. The shake is thanks enough."

"No, I insist. J.P. and me are driving up to The Needles after church tomorrow to do some climbing. Want to come? We're taking J.P.'s dad's car. That in itself is worth the trip."

Richard looked at him as if he were crazy. "With you two? Do you think I'm out of my mind?"

Tyler raised an eyebrow.

"Okay, I withdraw the question. But let's face it, Ty, you two have absolutely no sense of self-preservation. You act like it's some contest between the two of you to see who can kill himself first. No, you two go ahead and take the Bentley up to—"

"It's a Prowler. A Dodge Prowler. The coolest car—"

"Yeah, whatever. Take it with my blessings and knock yourselves out, which is probably exactly what you will do, now that I think about it. Wear a helmet."

They drove in silence for all of 10 seconds, and then Tyler said, "No, seriously, Richard. This thing with Hannah and Jessica—"

"Tyler, my friend," Richard said, slurping the last of his shake, "You're being cruel. I haven't even been on a date in three months. Ask somebody else."

Somebody else. Good idea.

"Talk to—you know. What's his name," Richard said. "Allen. The guy that used to be your youth pastor."

Just what Tyler had in mind.

chapter

ColoradoTy: hey old man. you just log on? how you doin? kids ok? kathy?

AllenOlson: Kids ornery as ever. Jason broke his arm falling off his bike, but he's okay. Kathy's teaching piano and up to her ears in local music activities, you won't be surprised to learn. Now, since you never ask about the fam except as a diversionary tactic, what did you really want to talk about?

ColoradoTy: okay, here's the thing. this guy, let's call him jimbo, had this girlfriend but she moved away so that's all over. this new girl moves to town, he starts to like her. then all of a sudden the old girlfriend moves BACK. and jimbo kind of likes them both but he doesn't want to be a creep or anything so how should he handle this if he's a christian?

AllenOlson: So how IS Jessica?

ColoradoTy: lookin good! we didn't really get to talk yet, though. and if i'm correctly interpreting the vibes, the girls don't seem to like her any better than last year.

AllenOlson: Well, I think your three amigas (or is it four now, with the addition of the lovely Hannah?) have pretty good judgment, so listen to them.

ColoradoTy: but i also remember you didn't really like jessica all that much yourself, so i'm thinking, are you agreeing with the brio team because that's right and fair, or because you just don't like her and it bugs you that she's back? people change—you taught me that.

AllenOlson: Fair question. And I see you're still the compulsively fair-minded person you have always been. But get one thing straight—it has NEVER been that I didn't LIKE Jessica. I like her fine, and wish her well. My concern was, I just didn't think she was mature enough and spiritually aware enough to help move you up, instead of down. You're right, people change. But I go back to my first comment. Your three Brio friends have good instincts about these things.

ColoradoTy: your point?

AllenOlson: Don't rush into anything. Get to know Jessica again slowly, as a friend. See if the changes you think you see in her are genuine. And even then, think long and hard about what kind of influence she'll be in your life before you get into anything more romantic with her. Remember, you have these great relationships with Jacie, Becca, and Solana—long-term friendships, very healthy, very balanced. Why would you want to threaten that by jumping into a quick romance? Take some time to figure things out. Hey—

why not bring Jessica into that circle? Make her a Brio girl!

ColoradoTy: allen, man, you're showing your age. you really think J, B, and S would appreciate me trying to shoehorn jessica, who they don't really much like anyway, into the group? hannah seems to be working her way in, but not because of me—the girls reached out to her on their own.

AllenOlson: Okay, good point. But ask yourself: Why don't they like her? Isn't it because last time you and Jessica got romantically involved, it almost split up the group? Jessica didn't like you spending time with them, and they were jealous of her, and they didn't think she was good enough for you. As I recall, it was Jacie in particular who was really hurt by what was happening between you and Jessica.

ColoradoTy: you haven't answered my question. i see jessica and i feel these old feelings cropping up. and then i look at hannah and i still feel everything i've been feeling for her all school year. so how am i supposed to handle all this?

AllenOlson: Not sure what you mean by 'handling' it. If you mean spending time with one or the other or both, I vote for both. Nothing wrong with dating more than one girl at the same time, Ty, buddy. You don't have to be exclusive. As long as both girls know that you're not in the market for a steady girlfriend, I don't see the problem.

ColoradoTy: trust me on this, allen. when you take a girl on a couple of dates, she thinks you belong to her, and she won't want you dating anybody else. i predict major fireworks.

AllenOlson: If I sound like I'm warning you away from

dating, that's not what I'm trying to do. The whole 'falling in love' scene is something ordained by God. Yeah, sure we blow it much of the time and make it look like something created by somebody else, but the truth is, feeling romantic attraction for someone is how God created you to feel. An important and healthy part of life. I mean, look at me—I'm madly in love! But be careful—don't let dating become more important to you than close friendships at this point in your life.

ColoradoTy: ok. but have you ever known me to do that, what you're saying?

AllenOlson: Well—okay, just that one time. With Jessica. And I guess that's why I'm a little concerned here this time. She's ba-a-ack.

● ● ●

Wincing a little at the pain from his scuffed and slightly bleeding knuckles, Tyler pulled himself up onto the limestone knob. He grinned at J.P., who was already there, leaning back against the rock and sucking at his water bottle. Tyler stood, letting the wind whip his hair around his face. "Oh, yeah," he said slowly, eyes closed, arms outstretched. "Man, that's good."

The sky was cloudless and deep blue, the air crisp and cold, with the distinctive smell of late autumn in the Rockies. Tyler was glad he had his long-sleeved, two-layer, polyester climbing shirt on under his climbing parka.

He opened his eyes. To the west, mountain range after snow-topped mountain range stair-stepped back into the distance toward the Continental Divide. The white trunks of the bare aspen almost glowed against the dark green spruce, pine, and fir in the afternoon sun.

They had begun climbing in a stand of larch directly below, bare-branched now, but Tyler remembered how they'd looked the last time he and J.P. had climbed here—covered with golden-orange needles.

"Did you know the larch is the only 'evergreen' tree that drops its needles in the fall?" J.P. asked, as if reading Tyler's thoughts.

"Duh," Tyler said, sprawling beside J.P. on the rock and reaching into his fanny pack.

"Just thought you might be interested in natural history."

Tyler took his sunglasses off and pulled a granola bar and his water bottle out of his pack. "J.P., no offense, but natural history isn't exactly your field, unless it has to do with football, baseball, or basketball."

"Or females," J.P. said and whapped Tyler on the knee, then pointed off to their right. About a hundred yards away and a couple dozen yards lower than the knob J.P. and Tyler sat on, two slender girls in tight, bright climbing outfits were scaling a rock face.

"I saw them getting their gear out of their car, back in the parking lot," Tyler said.

"Our age?"

"My guess is, freshmen or sophomores in college."

"Like I said," J.P. winked, "our age. Hey—did they see us by the Prowler? They'll know we're cool if we drive a Prowler. They might even want a ride."

Tyler shook his head. "Come on, man. We came here to scramble."

"We are. Hey—speaking of females, there's this crazy rumor flying around that one Jessica Abbott has returned to the city of her youth and to the arms of her one true love."

"Where'd you hear that?"

"Is it true?"

"Can't believe everything you hear."

"So it's true, then. The old Tyler/Jessica thing heats up again—"

"Whoa, not so fast." Tyler unwrapped his granola bar and bit off a piece. "Yeah, she's back. But that's it, so far."

"Go get 'er, man. She's hot."

Tyler shook his head. "J.P., I mean, listen, we're both guys and everything, but for your own good I've got to tell you that you need to start looking at girls as something more than sex objects. They have minds, they have—"

"Listen, Ty, you forget who you're talking to. I know what they have. I've been there. You haven't. And despite all of his brave talk about girls' minds, my friend Ty here has never dated an ugly girl in his life—am I right?"

Ty opened his mouth to respond, then stopped. It was true, after all. He picked his dates mostly because of their looks. Just like J.P.

"So she came back fat or something, then?" J.P. asked. "Is that the problem?"

A magpie, blackest black and whitest white, landed in a treetop just 20 yards away, cocked its head at them, and squawked.

"No, not at all. She looks—she looks—outstanding. Better than before, even."

"Unreal." J.P. nodded thoughtfully. "Because she was truly gorgeous a year ago. You were a lucky dude back then. Which raises the original question, which you have tried unsuccessfully to evade: Are you two going to get back together?"

The magpie squawked again and took off over their heads. "What are you talking about, man?" Tyler asked. "She's been in town since Wednesday, I've seen her exactly once, and you expect me to have our future all planned out? What, you want a wedding invitation?"

"No, because getting married would be really stupid. Don't tie yourself down, Ty—no pun intended. Pass me the binoculars."

Tyler pulled the binoculars out of his pack and handed them to J.P. He focused them on the girls climbing below them. "No, I was asking whether you're going to claim her. Because if you don't, I might take a shot at her myself."

Tyler felt an odd surge of feeling. Jealousy? Protectiveness?

J.P. lowered the binoculars and looked at Tyler. "Don't look at me that way, man. Most natural thing in the world. She's hot, so yeah, I'm interested. But you had her first, and I'm your bud, so you get first crack at her. You decide to pass, then it's my—"

"She's not a hamburger, J.P." Tyler felt some stiffness beginning to creep into his muscles. He stood and moved around to loosen up. "You're like, 'You gonna eat that?'" he said in a mock-Neanderthal voice. "'Cause if you ain't gonna eat it, I want it.' You know, she has a mind of her own. What if she doesn't want to go out with you, J.P.?"

J.P. stood and buckled his fanny pack. "Gee, I don't know. Never had that happen before." J.P. put his sunglasses on, looked at Tyler, and grinned. "You know something, Tyler? And I mean this in the nicest possible way, since you're my friend and all. But *you're* the strange one. Not me. If a babe like Jessica Abbott came back into town and wanted to hook up with me, I wouldn't have to think too long about it. And if I could talk her into the backseat—yeah, I'd do that. But, Tyler—so would any other guy at school, if they had the chance. Any other guy except you. *You're* the one whose attitude about girls is just a little bit weird, if you know what I mean. You want to protect Jessica Abbott's virtue—if she has any—then be my guest. Tell me she's yours, and that's all you got to say." He smiled, white teeth flashing. "See—I can be a nice guy. Now let's climb. Up this way." He pointed.

Tyler shook his head. "Not that way. We tried that route once

opportunity knocks twice

23

before and had to turn back." He pointed up. "Straight up this way, man. New route, some little overhangs—looks fun."

J.P. shook his head, still grinning. "This way has an obvious advantage. It will bring us out—" He pointed. "Right over there. And those two girls, when they get to the end of the route they're climbing, will come out—oh, look, bless my soul. They'll come out right over there too." He began to feel for handholds. "Now *that* is fun climbing. Besides, when we had to turn back—what was that, six months ago? We're better now. We can make it. Come on."

Tyler stood watching his friend spider his way up the rock face. But he wasn't thinking about the route. He was thinking about what J.P. had said about Jessica.

It didn't bother Tyler that, as J.P. had pointed out, his attitude toward girls was different from most guys'. Tyler firmly hoped that *most* of his attitudes were different from most people. The one thing Tyler never wanted to be was ordinary. And beyond everything else, he wanted to relate to girls in a way that was consistent with his faith in Christ.

"Hurry up, man!" J.P. called from high above. "Those girls are quick! If you don't get movin', they'll be gone by the time we get there."

What would he say when he and J.P. met up with the girls climbing the rock? They *were* pretty good-looking. But Tyler wasn't going to lie about his age. In fact, he wasn't into the whole pickup scene.

"Oh, baby!" J.P. hollered down. "Check out the one in orange! I got dibs!"

No, Tyler definitely did *not* want J.P. going after Jessica.

chapter

Tyler breezed into the kitchen on Monday morning and kissed his mom on the cheek as she stood at the counter brewing coffee. He flopped onto a stool at the breakfast counter. "Bring me food, woman," he growled.

"He really wasn't very specific," little sister Tyra said, dancing in barefoot, still in her sleep T-shirt. "Give him dog food." Tyra danced everywhere—that was the only verb Tyler could think of to describe her movement, so light, energetic, happy. It seemed to Tyler that only her toes ever touched the ground, and those only barely. It had been that way since she was tiny, and it was still true of her at 13— although, Tyler thought once again with concern, as he did every day, she could pass for at least a couple of years older.

"Dog food it is," his mom smiled, pouring her coffee, "but he's still going to have to get it himself. And you, young lady—you're still not dressed. Are you aware that you have to leave in 15 minutes?"

"Could you iron my pink shirt, Mom?" Tyra asked. "I wanted to wear that with my khakis and my—"

"Oh-ho," Tyler teased, "I can't ask Mom to get me my breakfast, which would take only a minute, but it's okay for you to ask her to iron—"

"Sorry to disappoint you both," their mom said, "but I've got to leave the same time you do, and I have to gather up some things first. So Tyler, get your own breakfast, something reasonably healthy, please, and Tyra, find something else to wear. And quickly."

"Mo-om," Tyra whined. Tyler grinned. At least she still whined like a little girl, even if she no longer looked like one.

"You could have ironed it yourself last night if that's what you wanted to wear," their mom said. "Too late to think of it now." She pointed back up the stairs. "March."

Tyra flounced away. Tyler dug through the pantry, then pulled a bag of toaster waffles out of the freezer.

"Have you talked to Jessica since the shoot on Saturday?" his mom asked as he poked the waffles into the toaster.

Here it comes. "Uh, no. Thought about it, but I didn't have her number."

His mom nodded, although both of them knew that he could have gotten the number if he'd wanted to, but hadn't because he didn't know what to do about Jessica, or even what to say to her.

"How did you feel about seeing her again?" She bit into a blueberry muffin.

Tyler shrugged. "It was weird. I wish I'd known ahead of time she was going to be there."

She sipped the steaming coffee. "She could have let you know. Somehow. I suspect that she wanted you to be surprised—shocked, even. Makes a stronger emotional impact that way."

Tyler didn't respond. The waffles popped up, and he spread margarine across them and then dumped raspberry yogurt on top.

"I have to admit I wasn't all that happy to see her," she continued. "I kept wondering what was going to happen—"

Tyler held up his hand. "Mom."

She looked up.

"I understand what you're saying," he said. "But I really don't like it when you talk about her that way."

His mom cocked her head. "What way? I'm not accusing her of anything, Tyler."

"Well, not yet, maybe, but we both know that's where it's going to end up. You always—" He stopped, then looked at his plate. He knew he was overreacting. She really hadn't said anything against Jessica yet. He pushed the yogurt around with his fork. "You remember all the fights we had about Jessica last year?"

"How could I forget?" she said, but there was a smile in her voice.

"Well, let's try something different this time. Let me figure out what's happening with Jessica. I'll keep you up-to-date. Really, I will. We can talk about it. But I need for you not to bug me about her, and not to dump on her either. You know—she might have changed. People do. It's been a year."

She studied him carefully. He felt a little self-conscious stuffing huge mouthfuls of waffle and yogurt into his face while she watched him. Finally she nodded.

"Yes. People do change." She took another sip, then stood, walked to the sink, and rinsed out her cup and dish. "All right." She kissed him on top of the head. "You'll really keep me up-to-date?"

Tyra rushed in and pulled the refrigerator door open. "Up-to-date on what?"

"None of your business," Tyler groused. Then he said to his mom, "Yes, I will. Promise."

She squeezed his shoulder. "Okay. We'll talk more later. Now you two need to scoot."

Tyra was bolting down a glass of milk. "This is all I have time for, Mom."

"Take a granola bar. Eat it on the way."

"Mo-om . . ."

"Don't argue! I have to run." She hurried into the study; they could hear her throwing things into her briefcase.

"When will Dad be back?" Tyler called.

"Friday, I think," his mom called back. "Unless he's delayed."

Tyler and Tyra exchanged a look. Their dad was often "delayed" on his business trips. And sometimes he showed up earlier than expected. They really never knew when he'd suddenly reappear from his trips. Tyler rinsed his plate and stuck it in the dishwasher.

"Are you ready to go?" Tyra asked. "Because I can't be late today." Tyler always dropped Tyra off at middle school on his way to Stony Brook High.

"Just have to gather up my books and stuff."

"Well, would you go do it please, because I need to go right now."

Tyler started up the stairs. "Who was it who couldn't manage to get dressed—"

"I'm ready now!" she yelled. "I'm ready! Right now!"

"You two stop it!" their mother called. "I'm leaving!" She made kissing noises. "Love you both. Be good. And don't be late! Tyler, you hear me?"

"Okay, Mom!"

The door to the garage slammed, and Tyler grabbed his backpack off his desk and began shoving things into it. By the time he'd found everything, though, it was five minutes after they should have left, and Tyra was buzzing like an angry mosquito all the way to school.

● ● ●

Tyler had known that, somehow, he and Jessica would end up together that day, and the time came during lunch. As he tossed his trash into the barrel and started to walk out of the cafeteria with Richard and Nate, there she was, standing against the wall, smiling at him.

"You guys go on ahead. I'll catch up," he said.

Richard raised a questioning eyebrow, then noticed Jessica. "Ah," he said.

Richard motioned toward her with his head for Nate's benefit, and Nate said, "Ah."

"Ah," the two of them said together.

Tyler propelled them toward their destination with a healthy shove on each shoulder. Then he found a spot against the wall next to Jessica, who regarded him with that amused smile he always found comforting and cute—the one that said she'd seen everything that happened, understood it, and it didn't bother her. That was, in fact, one of the things he had always valued about their relationship last year—that no matter how worried Tyler might be about something he'd done or said, it rarely bothered her. Almost without exception, Jessica was someone who just shrugged things off, more amused than angry. She seemed to be that rare exception to the rule—a girl whose feelings weren't easily hurt.

So when her amused smile changed into a pouting one, he just smiled. "I thought you'd call," she said.

"Hey, I'm still in shock," he said, reverting to the quiet, intimate voice he'd seldom used with anyone but her. He'd almost forgotten about that, and it surprised him that it so easily and automatically came back now that they were face-to-face and as alone as two people can be in a high school hallway.

She nodded, kept her pout for a moment longer, then sent him a flashing, toothpaste-ad smile that made his heart beat faster. "All is forgiven."

He reached into his pocket and found a scrap of paper. "For future reference," he said, handing it to her with the pen from his pocket.

She wrote her number on it and handed it back. "We'll be there until Daddy finds a place he wants to buy. This is just rented."

There was little doubt who made the decisions in Jessica's family. Her father was a vice president of a large company and was used to people doing what he said. Jessica's mother had tired of it long before and divorced him, and had been followed by a procession of Jessica's stepmothers, who had never managed to stay more than a year or two. Tyler was curious whether Jessica had the same stepmother now that she'd had when she'd left a year ago.

He stuffed the paper into his pocket and the two of them simply stood, smiling and leaning against the wall. Which seemed very comfortable. Tyler felt no pressure to launch into conversation.

"I don't know," she said at last, with a little laugh.

"Don't know what?"

Her smile broadened. "What's going to happen between us. I don't know whether you're dating anyone—and by the way, I didn't have anything serious going with anyone in Cleveland, no one I'm going to be writing to or anything like that."

"I find that hard to believe," he said.

She shook her head and tapped his chest with two fingers. "They just don't make them in Cleveland like they do in Colorado. Anyway, I can tell you *one* thing that will happen now. We'll be great friends, as always. Two people who know each other very, very well and can talk to each other about anything, and who always know that they'll be accepted and loved and supported. That much I know. If there's anything beyond that, as there was before—" She raised an eyebrow to show that the idea intrigued her. "We'll see."

"Here they are," came a voice Tyler had grown to love, and Hannah came smiling down the hall.

He felt Jessica's hand slip around his arm as she slid a couple of inches closer on the wall. She pulled his arm against her side. Tyler cocked his head and looked at her. Interesting. Was she staking a claim? But Jessica was concentrating on Hannah.

"I was *so* glad to find out you two were friends," Hannah said. "That must make it easier for you to fit back into things here, Jessica. Of course you must have a lot of friends here. It seems like everyone knows you."

Jessica smiled. "It's pretty easy to make friends here."

Hannah rolled her eyes. "I'm still feeling like an outsider, except with Tyler and his friends. I'm just not used to all this." She swept her arm around to indicate the school. "I feel like I never know what to say. Or if I do say something, that it comes out all wrong."

Jessica shook her head. "Believe me, Hannah, you have nothing to worry about. You have what it takes."

"You think so?" Hannah said, and Tyler couldn't help but smile. Yes, it was true. There *was* something the rest of them understood that Hannah, in her innocence, didn't. What Jessica had meant was that Hannah had a tall, slender, shapely body and blonde-goddess looks. And that *was* enough to make it in your average American high school.

And Hannah didn't have a clue.

Jessica smiled, squeezed Tyler's arm briefly, and then drifted away in the hall traffic.

As soon as she was gone, a worried look washed across Hannah's face. "Oh, Tyler—I hope your mom wasn't too upset that I brought Jessica to the shoot without asking first. I never even thought about it, and then when we got there she seemed a little—"

"It's best to ask," Tyler explained. "She likes to choose the models herself, that's all. Just give her a call first. No big deal. She was okay."

Hannah smiled. "I know. She's always okay. I love your mom."

"Everybody does," Tyler smiled ruefully, closing his eyes. "You have no idea how big a burden that can be."

● ● ●

As soon as the last bell rang that day, Tyler glanced at the note Solana had stuffed into his hand before his last class—"Come to Alyeria right after school, BEFORE basketball workout"—and jogged toward the "secret hiding place" he and the three Brio girls—Becca, Jacie, and Solana—had shared since their grade-school days.

He hadn't been surprised to get the note. Not after the photo shoot last Saturday. And in one way he couldn't blame the girls for being upset about Jessica. It *had* been hard on the group when he and Jessica had been dating a year ago. Tyler's loyalties had been divided. The Brio girls wanted him to spend time with them—which, of course, Jessica had resented, since she wanted him to spend time with her. So no matter who he was with, them or her, somebody somewhere was upset with him. His stomach had churned a lot during those months, and he hadn't liked himself very much. As he jogged up to the screen of bushes that hid Alyeria, hearing quiet voices filtering out from behind them, he made himself a promise: No matter what happened between him and Jessica this time, he wouldn't let either her or the Brio girls place those kinds of demands on him again.

Becca, Solana, and Jacie were perched on the little log benches they and Tyler had long ago dragged into their hiding place. Jacie, as usual, looked cold and was hunched into her black sweater, leaning against Solana for warmth, hands withdrawn into the sleeves. The three of them stopped talking as soon as Tyler came in, and all looked at him, but no one spoke—which didn't seem like them at all; usually they all talked at once.

He lifted his hands questioningly. "What?"

"Oh, hey, Mr. Impatience," Solana said.

"Come on, I've got to get over to basketball workout. Coach boils us in oil if we're late."

"Well, you know what it is, Tyler," Becca said. "We wanted to talk to you about Jessica."

"Yeah, okay," Tyler said warily. "What about her?"

"See, I told you," Solana said. "Already he sounds defensive."

Tyler shook his head. "No, no, I'm not defensive at all. In fact, I was glad to get your note because I wanted to tell you what Jessica and I had decided. We haven't set a date or anything yet, but we're both real clear on one thing. We want all three of you to be bridesmaids. Jessica has these really cute dresses picked out. You'll all be in peach, and Hannah—she's the maid of honor—she'll be in burgundy. You'll have—"

"Ha-ha," Becca said. "See how we're all laughing?"

"Well, what did you want me to say, Becca?" Tyler asked, laughing uneasily. "Look, I don't *like* being on the defensive, but that's how I feel. You've . . ." He stopped to think for a moment; the girls sat silently, watching him. "Look," he said, "let's start over. Just a minute."

He stepped outside of the hiding place, took a couple of deep breaths, and stepped back in again.

"Hey!" he said smiling. "Got your note. Look, I'm glad you asked me to come over. I've only got a minute because of basketball, but I wanted to talk to you about the Jessica situation. Just a couple of things first, and then you can ask me whatever you want. First, I don't know what's up with that. She just got here; I've talked to her exactly twice, once at the photo shoot where you all were, and then again for five minutes at school today. That's it. Second, you guys are my closest friends. I know we had some tension when she was here a year ago. I don't want that to happen again any more than you do. So let's make a deal—we *all* date people from time to time, so let's agree that we all have to have the freedom to do that without it messing up the group dynamics, so to speak. 'Cause I don't really want to feel torn between you guys and a girlfriend again."

"Or how about torn between two girlfriends?" Solana muttered.

Tyler shrugged.

"It's just that . . ." Jacie's voice trailed off as she struggled to put it into words. "Well, we remember how Jessica got really demanding and jealous, and we felt like she tried to turn you against us. We don't want that to happen. You're important to us, Tyler."

Tyler felt his hackles beginning to rise. "First of all, I don't think Jessica was the only one who was demanding and jealous. I think you guys worked just as hard to turn me against her."

"Hey, don't flatter yourself, amigo," Solana said. "We were never jealous. We were just doing you a favor. We could see what was happening, and we were trying to save you—"

"Solana, what do you say to us when we try to tell you we're concerned about your romantic life?"

She blinked. "What *do* I say?"

"You tell us to mind our own business. Sometimes not in those exact words," Tyler said. "I've got to admit, I think you guys are meddling."

"But this could affect all of us, Tyler," Becca said. "As best friends, we ought to have the freedom to tell you what we think."

Tyler closed his eyes and took a deep breath. He wanted to walk out, but somehow he couldn't. He shared too much with these girls. "Okay," he said resignedly. "I said you could ask some questions, didn't I? Ask away."

Silence.

He opened his eyes. The girls seemed uncomfortable, looking at the ground, at each other, then back at the ground.

"Well . . ." Becca began, and then stopped.

"Do you *think* you'll date her?" Jacie asked, nearly in a whisper, and she seemed frightened of what she might hear.

Tyler paused, then said, "Yeah, if I have to guess, I'd say we'll at least go on a few dates." He studied Jacie carefully. She seemed to shrink in on herself a little.

"Is she going to be good for your faith, Tyler?" Becca asked. "Will she push you closer to God, or pull you away?"

Hmmm. "You know, I was talking to Allen on-line last night, and he talked about that too. But I guess I haven't really thought about it much."

"Well, you should."

"Yeah. I should. But, I mean, if I thought that was a threat, then I wouldn't even . . . you know . . ."

More silence.

"I guess, really," Solana said, more subdued, "we just wanted to see how *you* were feeling about . . . things."

Slowly, Tyler smiled. Becca looked up, grinned crookedly, and chuckled a little. "All right. Here's how I'm feeling about . . . things." He stepped forward a couple of steps and planted a little kiss on the top of the three girls' heads, Becca first, then Solana, then Jacie. He stepped back and leaned against the branch. "And nothing's going to change that, all right? Here's my guarantee: If Jessica and I *do* start to date again, then the four of us will work hard and find some way to not let it come between us."

Jacie looked up, pain still evident on her face. "I don't know, Tyler. That may be harder than you think."

"Not if we all agree to make it happen. We can find a way, Jacie. We can. We've survived worse."

"Oh, yeah?" Becca said. "What?"

"Well, that's easy," Tyler answered. "For instance, we—" He lifted his watch suddenly and looked at it. "Oh, man, I'm going to be late. Coach'll kill me. Hey, I've got to run. But we'll talk again soon, okay? Hey, thanks for inviting me!"

As he turned, pushed his way through the bushes, and jogged away, Tyler grinned at the sound of their voices behind him, complaining about him leaving before they'd finished the conversation. But at least they were laughing as they complained, which meant they were in a better mood than they'd been in when he got there.

Maybe that's the real conflict, he thought, *Jessica on one side, the three of them on the other. Like last time. Maybe Hannah doesn't even figure into this tug-of-war. Because I don't know yet if she's even interested in picking up one end of the rope.*

chapter 4

"No! You kiddin' me?" Jason's words, so loud and so close to Tyler's ear, almost made him wince. Towel-drying his hair, Tyler grinned. He loved basketball, but one of the things he loved most wasn't the game. It was this—the locker room afterward: humid, a little smelly, but filled with loud guys who'd just worked hard together as a team, and who had earned the right to laugh, tease, talk, and horse around. Yeah, the talk got raunchy at times, which made Tyler uncomfortable. It was the teasing, the play, the friendship-building that he liked best.

"You're goin' out with Amanda Blume Friday? How'd you manage that?"

Tyler turned and saw that Jason, dressing right next to him, was talking to Brian Miller. Redheaded Brian, grinning, shrugged as he pulled on his socks. "Just asked her, man. I been leadin' up to it for a couple weeks, talkin' to her at lunch, stuff like that."

"Hey," Andrew said, walking past from the showers with his towel wrapped around him, "if you're takin' Amanda Blume out, take her to the *early* show. Leave lots of time before you have to take her home. She's hot. I know whereof I speak."

"That's the plan," Brian said, blushing a little. "I got a place in mind, up above the reservoir."

"No, come on, everybody goes there. She'll see all the other cars and freeze up," Jason said. He grabbed his pants out of his locker. "Let me tell you a better place."

"Won't make any difference," Andrew said. "I took her up above the reservoir a month ago, and there were other cars there, and she never even noticed. She had her mind on, uh, other things. Hey!" Andrew screeched, as J.P. snapped his behind with a towel, and everybody laughed.

"No, seriously, man," J.P. said, "congratulations." He shook Andrew's hand. "Although, let's face it, you picked a pretty easy target. If you want to compete with the big boys, you got to pick one that hasn't already decorated the backseat of half the cars in the school parking lot." He dropped his shoes on the concrete floor and stuffed his feet into them.

"Come on," Brian said. "It's not like she's—"

J.P. laughed. "Oh, yes, it is. It's just like that. Look at the way she dresses, man. She's a walkin' advertisement. Little, short dresses, tight jeans, tight tops—come on. Don't tell me she's not dressing to let you know she's available."

Listening to their conversation, Tyler felt an odd sensation. He'd heard this kind of talk hundreds of times before—nearly every day in the locker room, really. And he was comfortable with his own standards and his own attitude toward girls, which were both very different from the rest of the guys. So why was this talk making him so much more uncomfortable today?

"Hey," Brian said, starting to sound defensive about his weekend date. "That doesn't mean anything, man. That could describe a few dozen other girls at school, too."

J.P. pointed at him, grinning. "You're catchin' on. You'll go far. They're advertising, man. They may say one thing with their mouths, but when they choose their clothes in the morning, they express exactly what they're *really* trying to say."

Ouch. It was an almost physical sensation, the rush of understanding that came to Tyler. And he knew why this conversation, in many ways so like the others he'd endured with only minor annoyance in the past, was making him intensely uncomfortable today. This time it was different. Because suddenly he was painfully aware that his own sister, Tyra, was now grown up enough that she, too, had a figure. And even though her clothes were definitely more modest than those worn by, say, Amanda Blume, Tyler still had found himself, more than once, uneasy about how much of Tyra's skin showed or how much of her figure was revealed by tight-fitting clothes as she danced out the door.

A frightening thought hit him: Were scrawny, pimply-faced middle-school boys, right now, having this same conversation in their own locker room—about Tyra?

Tyler gritted his teeth.

"Whoa," he said, loudly enough that everyone turned and looked at him. J.P., who'd been popping a stick of gum into his mouth, stopped with his mouth still open, the gum still between his fingers, halfway in his mouth. "Let's be fair here," Tyler said. "Do you really think, when a girl dresses in a way that turns you on, that's why she's doing it? I mean—do they even *know* how those clothes affect you?"

The guys continued to look at Tyler for a few seconds more, then looked at each other, then all started to laugh at the same time.

"Duh!" Jason said. "I mean—what, are you kidding? *Of course* they know how those clothes affect us. That is exactly why they wear them."

"Tyler, Tyler," J.P. said, now chewing energetically. "These are simple facts of life. Girls . . ." He gazed toward the ceiling with a far-away look in his eye, and gestured with both hands. He had a grinning, appreciative audience, and he knew how to play it. "Girls are like flowers. They like to put on bright, showy, provocative petals. Some choose one color, some choose another. Some have long, modest petals, others are short and sassy. But all of those flowers have petals for the same reason." He looked back down, right into Tyler's eyes. "To attract some bee to come pollinate 'em, baby."

The locker room erupted in cheers and laughter.

"For some," J.P. went on, "it's just a tease. Others mean it big time. But don't fool yourself, my friend. They are *not* ignorant of how their clothes affect you. When you walk out of here, girls will smile at you and wave. Know what they're thinking? They're wondering whether their clothes are drawing your eyes to the parts of their bodies they want you to be aware of."

Tyler was speechless. The silence stretched. Finally, turning back to his locker, he mumbled, "J.P., you are so full of it."

J.P. stepped closer and said quietly, "You can say that if you want. But you know and I know that I just spoke the absolute truth."

Tyler finished dressing in silence, thinking only of Tyra. And he didn't like what he thought.

And, as luck would have it, as Tyler walked away from the locker room, the first girl he saw was Hannah—the *last* girl he wanted to be talking to while thinking about whether girls dressed to draw his eyes to parts of their bodies.

Look at her face, Tyler urged himself as she looked up, saw him, and smiled. She was walking down the sidewalk toward him, a few books under one arm. *Just look at her face.* But despite himself, he was aware that, even though no one at their school dressed more modestly than Hannah—today, it was an ankle-length skirt with a baggy, long-sleeved shirt—the body beneath those clothes was slender and shapely and moved with a natural swinging grace that made you aware of her body despite the clothes.

"*Hi*, Tyler," she grinned.

"Hey," he said. They both stopped. There was a moment of awkward silence, neither of them knowing what to say.

"You just coming from basketball practice?" she asked.

He nodded. "Still a few weeks away from the first game—we haven't even had the last cut yet. But Coach is working us pretty hard. We have a chance to take districts this year, and he doesn't want to blow it just because we didn't prepare."

She looked puzzled, and shifted her hips to take the weight of the books.

Look—at—her—face.

"Take districts? What does that mean?"

"Uh—to be the district champion. First we have to win our league. Then we play the champions of all the leagues in our district. And if we win that, we go on to the regionals. Then comes the state tournament. I don't think we'll go that far, but we really could win our district. We've got a lot of returning starters, and we almost won last year."

"Oh." She still didn't look like she understood. Then she smiled and shrugged it away. "Well, you look like you're in good shape." Then she looked embarrassed, shocked at herself, as if she'd said something too personal.

"Coach makes sure of that," Tyler said. Then there was another awkward silence, and Hannah looked out across the campus. Why did he always stumble all over his tongue when he tried to talk to Hannah? He'd never had a problem talking to girls. In fact, he'd always felt a little smug and superior around guys who were afraid to talk to girls. Now this. Why?

Of course, the reason might be obvious: He'd never known a girl who was into the courtship thing. Usually, if there was a girl you liked, you talked to her, found out if she liked you at least a little bit, and then you asked her out. But what do you do with a Hannah? In the first place, Tyler couldn't tell if she liked him in a romantic sense. Sure, she *liked* him; she wanted to be friends. But was there more than that? And suddenly he realized something: If he could just know, for sure, that she would *like* to date him, that she *wished* he could be her boyfriend, he thought he could deal with the fact that they *couldn't* date.

She turned toward him and cut into his thoughts. "It must be nice for you that Jessica is back in town," she said, her usually wide-open expression strangely unreadable.

"Well," Tyler began, then paused, unsure how to respond. "Sure, I'm glad she's back."

Hannah locked her eyes on his, but they weren't displaying their usual warmth. "That's just about all I heard all day: Tyler and Jessica, Tyler and Jessica. Everyone was wondering when the two of you are going to get back together."

"What? I find out she's back on Saturday, this is just Monday, and there's already a betting pool going on whether we're going to get back together?"

"It wasn't *that* bad. And you have to admit, you kind of asked for it."

Tyler shook his head. *Not again. Has she been talking to my mom?* "What do you mean?"

"Well, would they be talking this way now if you hadn't been dating her last year? It's having that kind of relationship that causes the problems, Tyler. It's not God's plan."

He moved away a step and looked toward his car. "Thanks for your concern, Hannah. But I'm not in the mood for another courtship lecture."

Her face softened, and she reached out a hand toward him, then stopped just short of touching him and lowered it again. "I'm sorry, Tyler. Really. I only want what's best for you. I care about you. I mean," she blurted, "as a sister in Christ."

Why was it completely impossible, when talking to Hannah, to say something like, *That's nice, Hannah, but a sister is not what I want you to be. I want something a whole lot more romantic than that—like to hold you tight in my arms and share a nice, long kiss.* He turned back toward her and waited, and she continued.

"I guess I can see why you two would date. You and Jessica."

Hmm. "You can?"

"Yeah. Jessica's fun and lively—a little flamboyant. I mean—you can't miss her. She catches everyone's attention. And I mean that in a *good* way. You're both outgoing, confident . . . I can understand why you'd be attracted to each other."

That sounded like bad news to Tyler. If Hannah thought *Jessica* was a good match for him, then what kind of match did Hannah think she herself and Tyler would make? Because Hannah and Jessica couldn't be more unlike each other if they tried. "Well," he said, stalling for time until he got his bearings, "a lot changes in a year."

She studied him closely, waiting for more, but he didn't know what to say. "So," she began with some hesitancy, "do you think you'll date her again?"

He shrugged. "You're right—she *is* a lot of fun. But if I dated her, I'd want to make sure . . ." What was it Allen had said? "I haven't really decided if Jessica's the kind of girl—" *Just shut up, Tyler. You don't know what you're talking about.* "I don't know."

Hannah shifted her feet. "I like Jessica. I really do. But when I talk to her about spiritual things, she kind of skims right by it." She gazed into his eyes, looking deep. "I think . . . I think that, even if I *believed* in dating, I wouldn't want you to date Jessica."

Never in a million years, Tyler realized, would he ever have guessed that he and Hannah would be standing here having this conversation today. How far could he press this? "So . . . you would want me to date someone else instead?"

"If I thought dating was okay, yes."

"All right, so . . . hypothetically speaking, if you were okay with dating—"

"That's not very likely, Tyler, because even if—"

"No, no, I know. But let's just pretend. We know you don't think Jessica's the right girl for me, so . . . *if* you believed in dating, and *if* I asked you out, would you go with me?"

She looked almost shocked. She clutched her shirt at her throat with one hand, and—she was blushing! "With you? On a date?"

He chuckled. "Hey, just for make-believe." He waited. "Would you?" he prompted. "Because if you could go on dates, Hannah, I would ask you."

She giggled uneasily, then began to speak way too fast. "I don't know. I—I haven't thought about it because—well, you know how I feel about it, and how my dad feels. He definitely is *not* going to let me date, not even for a minute. He believes . . . and really—" She waved her hands for emphasis, widening her eyes. "Really, I agree with him. I really do. I think the pattern of courtship is a lot wiser and safer for kids who seek to follow the Lord. So I don't want to date. I want to be totally sold out to the Lord, and if that means I have to arrange my social life a little differently than most people, well then, I know that's what's best for me. And so I accept that.

"You're sweet, Tyler," she said with a quick and nervous smile, "but I need to get home or I'll be late. See you tomorrow!" And she was gone, hurrying with those long legs down the sidewalk.

Tyler watched her go, feeling a sudden cold wind whip his hair. And he felt more confused about Hannah than ever. Had she been telling him that she *was* romantically attracted to him? Isn't that why she blushed and got nervous? Or had she been telling him that she wasn't?

"Whoa," Jason said, coming up beside Tyler and watching Hannah walk away. "Nice."

Startled, Tyler turned and looked at him, annoyed by the look on Jason's face as he studied Hannah. "What are you lookin' at?" he said.

Jason smiled, but didn't take his eyes off Hannah. "Same thing you were lookin' at."

A rush of guilt. "I was—uh—just standing here thinking."

Jason nodded. "Mm-hmm. And I bet you were thinking the same thing I'm thinking."

His face hot, Tyler walked away, Jason's laughter following him down the sidewalk.

chapter

"Oh, sure, it has to be Cadwallader & Finch, doesn't it?" Tyler said as he and Jessica approached the store. Tyler wasn't sure a trip to the mall on a Wednesday night counted as a date, but if it did, then he guessed it hadn't taken them long to fall back into *some* kind of dating relationship.

Jessica turned toward him and stopped as if she'd heard something in his tone. "I like their clothes. Really. Don't you?"

Tyler turned so that his back was to the store, not sure why—did he think someone was listening? "Well, it's the whole catalog thing. I mean, if they want to have a colossally expensive clothing store, then okay. If people want to spend that much on clothes, great. But in their ads and in their catalogs, it's like they're trying to change the whole moral attitude of everybody under the age of 25. I mean, shouldn't models in a clothing catalog be wearing clothes?"

Jessica tilted her head at him as if he was missing the point. "Are they really trying to change anything? Aren't they just reflecting what most people our age already believe?"

Tyler shook his head. "Not me."

"Me either. You know that. But they're selling clothes, Tyler, not starting a religion. They present what most people want, because that's how they attract kids to the store. And . . ." She took his hand and led him toward Cadwallader & Finch. "Just buying a couple of shirts here doesn't mean I agree with their catalogs. C'mon. I've already got the things I want picked out. All I need to do is pay, and we'll be gone."

True to her word, she led him back out of the store less than five minutes later. As they strolled for a moment or two, Tyler felt an odd mix of emotions—some awkwardness and even embarrassment over his little sermon about the Cadwallader & Finch catalog, and some anger at himself for feeling that embarrassment. After all, he truly felt that the clothing chain was way out of line with those catalogs, not to mention the huge, sexy photos of mostly unclothed models hung around the store. So why should he feel embarrassed about saying so? He shouldn't! In fact, he was just drawing a breath to raise the issue again with Jessica when suddenly she turned, gasped, and grabbed his arm. "Tyler!" she said. "I forgot to tell you! I'm getting a new car!"

What? "A new car?" he said. "Wait. Your car is two years old. How much newer can you get? Do you realize what year my car is? I drive a—"

"No, that's not really my car," she explained. "That's our family car, kind of a spare. I mean, it's a nice car and everything, but when I go away to college in a couple of years, I'll need one of my own to take."

Tyler nodded. "Okay. But your dad's buying it for you now?"

"As a kind of reward for all this moving around," she said. "Actually, I didn't mind coming back here at *all*. But Daddy thought he should do something to make it up to me anyway, so next week I get a new Miata!"

Tyler could feel his mouth drop open. "You're getting a *Miata*? A *new one*?"

She nodded happily—and, Tyler was aware even in his shock, very prettily. "Next Wednesday. Isn't that neat?"

"Uh . . . yeah. It's just . . . I mean, a Miata. They're so . . . expensive."

"No, not really. It doesn't even cost half as much as Daddy's car." Yes, Tyler had seen her dad's car. A sporty BMW. "And you know my dad. He's got connections everywhere. Probably got a very good price."

"Yeah. Wow. That's great."

She poked him in the side. "What's wrong?"

"No, nothing's wrong—that's great. I just . . . it's hard for me to imagine, that's all. Your dad giving you a new car."

"Maybe your parents will give you one for graduation next year."

He laughed. "It wouldn't be a new Miata, that's for sure. Hey, you hungry?"

She squeezed his arm. "Not really. But we can eat if you are."

Tyler was in the mood for Chinese, and he headed toward the Panda Express in the food court. It wasn't his hunger he was most aware of as they walked, though. It was two things—one, the fact that the girl walking beside him, looking his way and smiling up at him occasionally, walking close and cozy, was definitely the best-looking girl in the mall tonight.

But the other thing he was aware of was the vastly different world she lived in. A world where it was no big deal to walk into a store like

Cadwallader & Finch and buy a couple of shirts not all that much different from those you'd buy at the Gap or someplace like that, but that cost 60 bucks each. Sixty bucks. *Each*. And to pay for them with Daddy's credit card. A world where parents bought brand-new Miatas for their daughters just because, someday, those daughters would go off to college and need a car.

A world where Daddy dumped his wife every few years and took up with a new one, prettier, younger. Half of Tyler, to be truthful, wished *his* dad would do the same, just so he'd be gone. But the other half wanted nothing more than for his parents to stay together, and for his dad to become a better dad, a better husband to Tyler's mom.

Tyler had spent a fair amount of time in Jessica's house before she'd moved. And it had always seemed like a foreign country to him, where they spoke a language he barely understood, and where the food and the customs were odd. And now two things in the space of a few minutes had reminded him of just how different he and Jessica really were.

"You know what I want to hear about, Tyler?" she asked, a few minutes later, as they sat over a plate of orange chicken and fried rice. She hadn't ordered anything; she just wanted to pick off his plate, so he'd grabbed two forks.

"The alarming health risks of monosodium glutamate in some Asian foods?" he asked.

"Later. Right now I want to hear about your music."

"Oh, I like Dido, Creed—"

She nudged him with her shoulder. He liked it that she sat so close to him as they nibbled off the plate together. "You know what I mean. Your own music. Are you writing? Do you ever get to perform anywhere? I know how important that used to be to you. Is it still?"

He popped a piece of orange chicken into his mouth, then talked around it as he chewed. "Yeah. I mean, I'm still writing stuff. I sing a little bit for our youth group sometimes. That's about it." He washed the food down with Dr Pepper.

She watched his face, waited for more. "But you'd like to do more?" she prompted.

He shrugged. "Sure. 'Course I would. But I've learned something about myself in the past year. I've listened to other performers, singers, bands, and I've discovered that I'm not a solo act." He scooped up a big forkful of pork fried rice. "I need a band to give my music more . . . more personality or something."

He saw his friend Doug walk by, in a hurry for something, not looking around, preoccupied. And right behind him, giggling and laughing among themselves, came the Brio team—Jacie, Becca, Solana. Normally, he'd have flagged them down, been overjoyed to run into them. But tonight, with Jessica . . . he really hadn't figured out the dynamics between Jessica and the Brio girls yet. Feeling a little guilty, he watched them go by.

"So you're putting a band together?"

He turned back toward Jessica. She was snuggled right up against him, her happy little face a few inches from his. "It's not so easy to get a band together. I've asked around, but haven't found anybody who wants to join. Not anybody good enough, anyway."

"But why not? Why wouldn't—"

"Because some guys want to play nothing but hard rock and get gigs at dances and stuff, others are into blues or reggae—I just want a great bunch of musicians who like the kind of music I write and can back me up and make my songs sound really good. And our musical styles have to mesh."

She studied him for a minute, brows knit.

"You want some more of this?" he asked, noticing that the plate was about empty.

She shook her head. He finished it off.

He was slurping the last of his Dr Pepper through the straw when she brightened and said, "Maybe I can help."

"How?"

"What kind of musicians do you need? Drummer? Piano player? Maybe I can help find them."

"Oh," Tyler said. "Well, yeah, a drummer, maybe somebody on keyboards. But if we have a good lead guitarist, might not need the keyboard player. And a bass player. That's it, really. Fewer the better."

She tilted her head back, seemingly lost in thought. "I know a bass player," she said. "I think he—"

"Well, well," came Solana's voice. Tyler heard chairs pulling out at the table next to them, and there were his three Brio sisters, holding cups of frozen yogurt. He felt Jessica's hand slip across his back, then up on top of his shoulder—light but definite.

"You're not eating, Jessica?" asked Becca, eyeing the one plate in front of Tyler. "Tyler too cheap to buy you anything?" He noticed Becca's eyes flash up toward Jessica's hand on his shoulder.

Jessica laughed. "I wasn't very hungry, but I stole a few bites of Tyler's." She held up her fork as proof.

"Whoa," Solana said. "Must be serious, if he lets her take food right off his plate and doesn't even leave scars."

"I'm still hungry," Tyler said. "Right now I have an overwhelming desire for—hmm, raspberry frozen yogurt with—my gosh—gummi bears on top?"

"Keep your mitts off my dinner," Solana said.

"Goodness," Tyler said. "Going to leave scars?"

"Hey, girls," Jessica said brightly. "Any more magazine photo shoots coming up? That was fun."

Tyler watched the split second of panic wash across the faces of the Brio girls and grinned.

"Nothing planned," Jacie said. "But Tyler always knows, since it's his mom."

Jessica leaned toward the three of them. "I don't know if she was that crazy about having me there. You think?"

Becca, Jacie, and Solana looked at each other. "She pretty much likes to choose her own models," Becca said. "I guess Hannah didn't know that."

"Oooh, Cadwallader & Finch," Solana said, noticing the bag in the seat beside Jessica.

Here we go, Tyler thought.

"You like their clothes?" Jessica asked, smiling.

"Not sure," Solana said. "I went in one day and they said, 'You're early—the cleaning crew doesn't start till the store closes at nine.' Then when I told them I wasn't on the cleaning crew, they thought I was trying to lift something and threw me out."

Jessica barked out a short laugh, but it faded quickly; she was probably unsure whether Solana was teasing. "Well," Jessica said, "if you think you might like their clothes, why don't you come by some day and borrow some of mine? I have lots of their stuff."

Solana looked down at Jessica's narrow hips, then at her own more ample ones. "Uh, you know what, Jessica?" she said in quiet, dangerous tones. "Why don't you—"

"So, Jessica," Becca quickly interrupted before Solana got started, "any more shopping to do tonight?"

Jessica smiled and shook her head. She held up the Cadwallader bag. "This is all I came for. And to steal lemon chicken off Tyler's plate."

"Orange chicken," Tyler said.

"Whatever. I'd like to stay and chat, but I have two chapters to read. Tyler—" She touched his hand and smiled up at him sweetly. "You ready to go?"

Who could refuse that face, that smile? Then he glanced up at Jacie, Becca, and Solana, and saw the disappointment on their faces. They'd been hoping to sit with him a while. He battled a moment with the decision—and then sighed. Here he was again, just where he'd vowed to himself he would not be: torn between his Brio friends and Jessica. "Well, actually," he said to Jessica, "couldn't you . . ."

A look of annoyance flitted across her face for a second. She looked out across the mall, noticed something, and her smile returned—but to Tyler, it seemed forced. "You don't have to run me home after all." She pointed as she stood. "I see Daddy coming out of the jewelry store. I can ride with him. But we're still on for this weekend," she said, looking directly at Tyler. "No excuses. See you tomorrow!" And then she was gone, walking quickly away, dark legs flashing beneath her short skirt. They all sat silently, watching her go.

"It's a real art," Solana said in grudging admiration, "twitching a skirt that way. Not as easy as it looks."

Tyler looked grumpily at the three of them. "Least you can do after that is give me a bite of your yogurt."

Jacie obediently handed him her cup. He looked in. Chocolate yogurt with crunched-up Snickers topping. His favorite—but he wondered why Jacie had gotten it, since she preferred fruit flavors. Oh well. He dipped the spoon in, sucked it off.

"Least we can do after what?" Becca asked.

"Scaring my date away." Tyler slurped the words around frozen yogurt. "I wanted to talk to her some more."

"Scaring her away?" Jacie asked. "How did we do that?"

"Solana had her claws out and was just about to pounce when Becca butted in. Don't think I didn't notice."

"*Tyler*," Becca said. "Didn't you notice what Jessica was doing to Solana?"

"What do you mean? She offered to share her clothes. She was being friendly."

The girls looked at each other.

"*What?*" Tyler said.

"Tyler," Jacie said, "Jessica was deliberately pointing out that she wears about a size three or something, while Solana wears ... well ..."

"Never mind what size I wear," Solana said darkly.

"Besides," Becca said, "you'll notice that she took the opportunity to point out that she had *lots* of very expensive Cadwallader clothes, while Solana can only manage to get kicked out of the store. Did you really, Solana?"

Solana just grinned.

"No," Tyler said, "no, I think you misunderstood what she was doing."

"Trust us on this, Tyler," Becca said. "This is a language that girls speak very well. We know what she was saying."

Tyler took another spoonful, then looked carefully at the three of them. "Is this going to be a problem? What we talked about on Monday?"

"Tyler," Becca said, "she was deliberately ..." She stopped herself, thought a few seconds, then started over. "Okay, forget what she said to Solana for a minute."

"Wish *I* could," Solana said.

55

"Think about the Cadwallader thing. How did you feel going into Cadwallader & Finch and buying clothes with her?"

Tyler hesitated, then said, "So you're saying it's impossible for a Christian to buy clothes at—"

"No, wait," Becca said. "I know how *you* feel about Cadwallader because we've talked about it before. So what I asked was, considering how you feel about the company and the catalogs and the whole thing, how did you *feel* walking in there?"

Tyler stared into the yogurt, stirring it slowly with the spoon.

"You don't need to answer," Becca said. "We already know."

"But that's just it, Tyler," Jacie said. "If you hang around with Jessica, every date is going to be filled with things that are a conflict for you. She just—she just lives in a different world from you."

Tyler shook his head. Weird. Almost the exact same words he'd been thinking himself a half hour ago.

"You going to leave any of that for Jacie?" Solana asked.

Tyler looked down at the yogurt cup in his hands. "Whoops. Sorry, Jacie."

"It's all right."

"No. That was bad. Let me buy you another one. I just got, uh, distracted."

"No, really. I had all I wanted. All I needed. Too many calories as it is."

"Oh, right," Solana said. "Look at you. Now look at me. Now which of us has to count calories? You probably *could* wear Jessica's clothes. Well, except you'd stretch her sweaters out right across—"

"*Sola*na!" Jacie complained, embarrassed.

"Well, if you don't want any yogurt," Tyler said, "let me buy you some jewelry. Please. I'll feel better."

"Jewelry for me, Tyler?" Jacie asked.

"For all three of you. I'm feeling generous tonight, and besides, I only had to buy one dinner. But forget the jewelry store Jessica's dad came out of. I happen to know a store just a few doors down from here that has bracelets and necklaces and rings in stunning shades of orange and pink and purple, only the highest quality plastic. You deserve the best."

"Finally he has realized our true value," Solana said.

"Gee," Tyler said, "if your true value is a 25-cent ring, what would be the true value of a person who gets a red Miata?"

"A red Miata?" Becca said. "Great car—but what do you mean?"

"You'll find out," Tyler said as he stood and tossed the empty yogurt cup in the trash. "Next week."

● ● ●

ColoradoTy: here's what I'm wondering—what was it that first attracted you to kathy?

AllenOlson: For a minute I'll stop wondering why you're asking and give you a straight answer. First thing was, I just thought she was so doggone cute. Great smile that seemed to make the whole room light up, these bright, expressive eyes, cute little nose. I couldn't stop looking at her. We hadn't even been introduced, I didn't know her name, but—she was so happy! Well, come on, Ty, you know her—perkier than Kathie Lee Gifford. Irrepressibly cheerful and happy. I liked that. A lot.

So, sure, I admit it, first of all it was how she looked. That's why I got somebody to introduce us. But by the time we'd sat there and talked for a couple of hours that night, and I'd listened to her laugh (you've heard that laugh, Tyler—how can anybody hear that laugh and not become deliriously happy?) and gotten a glimpse of the person she was inside, I was hooked. I had to see her again. By the time I'd known her a week, I could have made you a long list of the things that fascinated me about her, from her musical talent to her strong drive to succeed to her love for the Lord to her big bright green eyes—well, you get the picture. Her looks caught my attention first, but there are lots of beautiful girls in the world. It was what I found in her after she got my attention that won me over.

ColoradoTy: that won YOU over? ha! not the way i heard it. she says you were the one doing the chasing, pal.

AllenOlson: Yeah, I pursued her until she caught me. So that's my story. Now, if I may ask, what's yours?

ColoradoTy: well, i've got this friend, let's call him bubba. he knows these two girls who are both pretty good lookers, the kind you don't want to stop lookin at, but good lookers in very different ways, like they were . . . okay, if they were models, one of them would probably be in cadwallader & finch ads, the other would have a milk moustache. you with me?

AllenOlson: I get the picture.

ColoradoTy: so these two are very much on poor bubba's mind. and he's aware that, just as they are very different in the looks department, they're also unlike each other in every other way—values, beliefs, social outlook, dress, character, tastes—lo, even as much as rebecca st james differs from jennifer lopez. if bubba wanted to go out on saturday night and have a really good time (wink, wink), he would know which of these young ladies to pick. in fact, he couldn't go out with the other one at all even if he wanted to, which he desperately does, because her dad doesn't support dating, being into the whole courtship thing, and that particular young lady, hard as it may seem to believe, actually sides with her dad on that one. so young bubba sits in confusion, regarding his options in the young lady department with obvious admiration but not the foggiest clue which of the two of them to choose. so he climbs the mountain and seeks out the dried up, wrinkled, ancient sage, places an offering of rice and trinkets at the old guy's feet, and begs for guidance.

AllenOlson: Well, the first thing the old guy would tell Bubba is, look, kid—you don't HAVE a choice.

ColoradoTy: explain please.

AllenOlson: Bubba is enamored of the fair Hannah, but Hannah cannot date. True? So even if Bubba decided that she was the one woman for him for his entire life—a decision Bubba is nowhere close to being able to make—there's nothing Bubba could do about it but sit around and mope. Hannah will not date, hold hands, kiss, go for long romantic rides in Bubba's limousine, or any of the other stuff Bubba might want to do with a girl on a Saturday night. So if he wants a date for the dance or the movie, he can choose Jessica, or he can choose some other lovely lass, but Hannah is off limits. Is that true, or is the Guru missing something?

ColoradoTy: well, yeah, but . . . i mean, there's got to be something bubba can do. talk to her dad? call in the national guard? disguise himself as a girl so her dad won't know she's going out with a guy?

AllenOlson: From Bubba's description, it doesn't sound to the Guru as if Hannah and her dad are likely to be talked out of what they fervently believe. Still Bubba has choices. He can forget about Hannah. Or he can continue to build a friendship with her, a nice nonromantic one, such as he has with the Brio chicks. Or he can fall in love with her anyway and make himself miserable. Option A is unworkable. And Option C is stupid. Let's see . . . that leaves . . .

ColoradoTy: bubba is not willing yet to give up on option d—sweeping her off her feet and somehow getting past the no-dating rule.

AllenOlson: Well, Bubba sounds like a determined young man, especially for someone who hasn't even figured out which of these tender young beauties he WANTS to date. But at the risk of sounding stern and unspeakably grownup, the Guru suggests that Bubba consider something: If Hannah believes that dating is wrong and harmful for her, and considers her stand against dating to be part of her commitment to God, then what kind of favor is Bubba doing for Hannah if he actually DOES talk her out of it and gets her to go out with him?

ColoradoTy: sounds like the guru is pushing bubba toward jessica, which would surprise him very much.

AllenOlson: Not exactly. He's trying to encourage Bubba to behave responsibly toward ALL his feminine companions, including those from the Brio squad. And with that in mind, just before the Guru bows out in response to the pull of his little children on his sleeve, calling him to dinner, he imposes upon Bubba this challenge: Imagine, if such a thing be possible for a young man, that he has married Jessica. Ten years from now, what will her influence upon his life have made him? Deeper, stronger, closer to God, a man of integrity and character? More materialistic, less interested in spiritual things, more sensual? Then he should project himself ten years into the future with Hannah as his wife.

How has she influenced him? Then he should bring the Guru another bowl of rice.

ColoradoTy: a thousand thanks, your alzheimeredness. and bubba sends his humble regards to the fam.

chapter

Tyler had tossed a bag of nacho tortilla chips onto the kitchen counter and was pouring a glass of chocolate milk when a load of books and papers slammed onto the counter beside the glass. He jumped, and the stream of chocolate milk missed the glass, splashing onto the counter.

"What is *that?*" barked his dad.

"Dad—that's my *homework!* Now you messed up—"

"I *know* it's your homework—what I want to know is why it was still spread all over my desk." Tyler's dad was only about an inch taller than Tyler. But he was heavier, solid—an imposing presence anytime, and especially now, radiating anger, scowling, his eyes piercing. But then, that's how he looked most of the time to Tyler.

"How many hundreds of times have I told you—if you want to do your homework at my desk, you sit down, you do it, you clean up after yourself, and you leave the desk just the way it was when you sat down. And how many hundreds of times have I found your homework still sitting there, like I did just now? I don't have time to clean up after you, Tyler! I have bills to pay tonight."

"Dad, I was doing my homework there when Mom asked me to set the table, so I got up and I did it. And then we ate—"

"Tyler, the last thing I want to hear is your excuses!" Tyler's dad was standing much too close as he yelled, as he usually did. It was as if he wanted to make sure he was within arm's reach if he needed to reach out and grab or slap.

"But I *don't* leave my homework there—"

"Don't interrupt! This is a very simple thing, Tyler. If you can't manage it, then do your homework in your room—it's such a disaster already, nobody would notice a little more clutter. Now do you understand that, or do I have to explain it in one-syllable words?"

Tyler picked up his English paper, due the next day. Chocolate milk dripped from the pages. "Dad—this is ruined. Now I have to—"

"I asked you if you understand me! Do you?"

Tyler dropped the wet pages in the trash. He would wait till later, when his dad was done paying bills, to print out a new copy. "Yeah."

"What?"

"Yes, sir. I understand."

"Good. Although why do I have this feeling that the next time I sit down to pay bills, I'm going to, once again, find your homework scattered all over?" He turned, took a couple of steps, then turned toward Tyler again. "And speaking of bills, I'd better not find a lot of long-distance calls on the phone bill when I open it. Last month there was 20 bucks' worth of calls to California, all of them to your friends. Am I going to find that again this time?"

Tyler tried to think, but as usual when he talked with his dad, his brain wasn't working very well. "Well—I don't know. I called my friends a few times. I mean—I mean, they're my *friends*. You have to keep in touch."

His dad looked as if that was the stupidest thing he'd ever heard. "You have to keep in *touch?* No, what you have to do, Tyler, is what you can afford to do. Period. And since you're not paying these bills, then I guess you'll have to hold your long-distance calls to what *I* can afford. And I can't afford much." He closed his eyes and pinched the bridge of his nose as if this conversation were giving him a headache. It was certainly giving Tyler a headache. "You want to call your friends in California," his dad said, eyes still closed, "then call 'em once a month. And keep it short."

"Once a *month?*" Tyler sputtered. "But they're my *friends!* I have to talk to 'em more often than that! I know *lots* of people in California, and I only see them—"

His dad held up a hand to stop Tyler's talk. His anger barely held in check, Tyler stopped in mid-sentence.

"If you're working such long hours and earning so much money that you can afford to pay for several long-distance calls a month to your friends in California, then by all means, call away. And then I'll expect you to pay me back for those calls when bill-paying time comes. But if you can't do that, then don't make the calls. You hear me?"

Seething, Tyler forced himself to stand still, not answering. The kitchen phone rang, but he knew better than to answer it—few things infuriated his dad like being ignored. And his dad didn't answer it either—when he zeroed in on Tyler, nothing distracted him.

"I said, do you hear me?"

"I hear you."

The phone didn't ring a second time, which was no surprise—

Tyra was home somewhere; she'd have leapt for the nearest phone as soon as it rang once.

"So what's that look?" his dad said.

Tyler shook his head. "No look, Dad. I'm, uh—I'm just bummed that I have to print my paper out again, that's all."

"Why should *you* be bummed? You're not paying for the paper. Next time, take care of your homework papers and nothing's likely to happen to them. Especially if you can keep from spilling the milk I paid for."

"Tyler!" Tyra poked her head in from the hallway. "Phone's for you. Jacie." She tossed the cordless; Tyler caught it.

"Tyra!" their dad snarled. "That's an expensive—do you—"

"Sorry!" Tyra called musically, and disappeared back up the stairs, humming.

"Hi. Just a minute," Tyler breathed into the phone, then looked at his dad. "Are we through?"

His dad locked eyes with him, scowling. He held the moment, and then waved dismissively. "Just don't forget what I said."

Tyler tucked the phone against his shoulder as he headed up the stairs. "Hey."

"Hey yourself. Whatcha up to?"

Tyler didn't answer till he had closed his bedroom door behind him. "Oh, a nice little father-and-son chat." He fell backward onto the bed. "Plus he decided to toss my English paper in the chocolate milk I spilled when he . . . oh, you know. The usual." He hadn't bothered to turn on the light. He didn't need it.

"Oh, Tyler. I'm so sorry. Didn't you say he was out of town?"

"Isn't he always? But he got home last night."

"So how are you feeling?"

Tyler shrugged, then realized that that was not a particularly eloquent way to communicate over the phone. "You know." He smiled then, knowing that Jacie was nodding. He could see exactly how she moved, the phone tucked against her shoulder, her right hand twirling a strand of her hair, eyes open but unfocused, concentrating entirely on her conversation, on him.

"Yeah," she said. "I know."

Tyler actually had his mouth open to say that the world would be a better place without dads, but he realized just in time that Jacie, who had grown up without a dad in the house, and who had often told him how she missed having her dad around, was not the best person to say that to. "It's just . . . I don't know. Forget it. What's up?"

"What do you mean, what's up?"

"Well—you called. What do you need?"

"Do I need a reason to call? Can't I just call you up and say, 'Hey, old bud, friend for life, honorary Brio Girl, fellow Alyerian, how are things?' And it sounds like I called at the right time."

If any of his guy friends had said that, Tyler would have laughed and said, "What do you need? A loan? A favor?" Guys called for a reason. But Jacie was probably telling the truth. "Yeah, good timing all right. You probably got me out of another 15 minutes over the flames. I think he was just about to slather a little more barbecue sauce on me."

"Remember: All good things must come to an end. A couple more years and you'll be off at college somewhere, sunning yourself next to some girl in a bikini and reminiscing about all those loving chats with Daddy."

"The operative word is *year*. A year is a long time. *Two* years looks like an eternity. You want the truth? I don't think we're going to be able to get through two more years of each other without some punches being thrown. Frankly, that doesn't sound like such a bad idea to me right now. And I don't think he'd really care either."

"Tyler..."

"We wouldn't be the first. Did you hear Brad Miller got into it with his dad the other day? He showed up at school with a black eye."

"Tyler..."

"I wouldn't even mind the black eye. It would be a badge of—"

"*Tyler.* I know you don't mean that."

"You don't think so?"

"You're not going to punch your dad. And you know why? Because your mom and Tyra would freak out. They love you, but you know what? They love him, too, in spite of who he is. And to have the two of you swinging away at each other, getting bloody noses or whatever, all that yelling, it would tear them apart. So get this through your head—no slugging. Give him dirty looks if you have to, but no slugging."

Tyler breathed deeply, let it out. "Yeah. I guess they—"

"And you want to know another reason?"

He grinned. "I think you're about to tell me."

"Because that's not the kind of person you want to be. The kind of person who punches out his dad."

"Or, more likely, gets punched out."

"Either way. Tyler, you're just like me, just like Becca. You *want* to do what's right, but most of the time it's hard because the things we want to do at any given moment just seem to be the opposite of what God *wants* us to do. Hey, just like Paul. 'For what I want to do I do not do—' "

"Yeah, yeah," Tyler interrupted, a little annoyed. "I know the verses." Why did this annoy him? He and Jacie had these kinds of conversations all the time. Ah—it was because that passage in Romans chapter seven that Jacie quoted was the very one Tyler had chosen for the devotions he'd given at the last youth group retreat. They were *his* verses. And he didn't much enjoy having someone else quote them to him as if he didn't know them.

"Well, okay, that's all I'm saying," Jacie went on. "All right. End of sermon. Sorry."

"You're forgiven." Tyler picked up his guitar and ran through a few lines from the song he'd been working on earlier in the week. Jacie didn't talk; Tyler knew she could hear him playing. Usually, when he played while they were on the phone, she just listened. Listened and waited.

"You doing okay?" she said after a minute or two.

How to answer? Girls were always asking how you felt about things. Half the time, Tyler didn't even know. How *did* he feel right now? He could usually tell someone what he *thought about* something, or what he was going to *do*—but how he *felt?* Maybe that's why he ended up shrugging so much when he talked to Jacie on the phone. "Well," he said at last, "I've had worse nights. Truth is, this is just life with my dad. I hate it. But this is how it's always been."

Tyler sensed that that wasn't a very complete answer, not what Jacie had been hoping for. But he was relieved when she didn't push for more.

"You know what you need?" she said brightly. "A Dr Pepper and some fresh air. You want me to swing by and get you?"

That did sound good, but . . . "Listen, Schweetheart," he said in his best Humphrey Bogart impression—which, he knew, was pretty bad. "You think I got time to mess around with dames? I got a load o' homework tonight, baby. More than a classy dame like you could do in a year. If I don't get it done tonight, heads are gonna roll. So thanks, baby, but duty calls."

A short pause, and Tyler could tell, when she spoke again, that she was disappointed. He was surprised. "Yeah, me too," she said. "Just thought it might make you feel better to talk."

"Hey, no, really," he said in a much more tender tone that he seldom used with Jacie, "it *did* make me feel better. I'm glad you called. Jacie, you *are* a sweetheart. Really. Hey, look at this smile! See how happy Tyler is? Just because you called!"

She laughed. "I'm glad. Tyler, I . . . I, uh . . . ha! I don't know what I'm trying to say. Hey, want me to dip your math homework in a strawberry malt, so you can have—"

"Grrrr . . ."

"Bye!"

chapter 7

"Hey, wow, man, look!" Jason said the next day as Tyler slid onto the bench at the lunch table where, it appeared, Tyler's whole basketball team was sitting. "Tyler Jennings is sittin' with us today. Call the channel 13 news, man!"

"Yeah, yeah," Tyler mumbled. "I sit with you guys at least a couple of times a week." The day was cool, but the sun was bright, and Tyler settled into his group, enjoying the chirps, squeals, and hum of several hundred teenagers taking advantage of a beautiful fall day to eat lunch outside.

"Oh, sure, whenever you aren't mobbed by girls," Doug said.

"Really, though, think about it," Brian said. "Tyler's got not just one girl hangin' around him all the time, he's got three!"

"Three?" Doug said. "Where you been? Add Jessica, you got four.

Now, the real question is: Will Tyler be able to add Hannah to his harem and make it five?"

"Why do I have this . . ." Tyler said, digging into the lunch sack he'd brought from home and pulling out a granola bar, "this incredible sense of déjà vu? Guys, we've gone over this before. Jacie and Becca and—"

"Yeah, yeah," Doug said. "We've heard it. Just friends. Now observe, compadres. Over yonder by the vending machines comes Solana, one of Tyler's 'friends.' Everybody wave. Hi, Solana!" Doug called, and everyone else at the table—everyone except Tyler, who could guess where Doug was going with this—waved and called or whistled. Solana grinned, waved, and wiggled her hips. The guys around the table hooted and yelled.

Why did you do that? Tyler wondered, shaking his head. He knew Solana well enough to know that that was how she teased, how she played. But he also knew what the rest of the guys around the table were thinking. He remembered J.P.'s words from a couple of days before: "They're advertising."

"Now," Doug continued. "I ask all of you. Is that anybody's 'just friends'?"

"No way!" came the answer.

"Yes way," Tyler said, munching on his granola bar. "Whether you believe it or not. You know what's wrong with you guys?"

"Yeah, and I know what'll take care of it, too!" somebody yelled, and the table erupted in laughter.

"What's wrong," Tyler continued, "is that *you're* so obsessed with sex, you think everybody else is too. So when a girl is friendly and outgoing, you think she's coming on to you. Do you have any idea how stupid—and egotistical—you look to a girl when you misunderstand her like that?"

"Are you talkin' about Solana?" Jason asked. " 'Cause that don't sound like Solana to me."

"What I'm saying about Solana," Tyler said, trying to ignore the concern that swept through him, as it so often did, when he thought of Solana and her partly earned reputation, "is that she's so much smarter than you guys when it comes to romance that not one of you boneheads is ever gonna get the better of her. When you're with Solana, you might *think* you're in charge. Ha."

"Hey, why get mad at us?" Jason asked. "We're not the ones with girls hangin' all over us. That's you, man."

"Good point," J.P. said. He hadn't been there a few seconds before, but now he slid his hip up on a corner of the table and perched there, sipping a Coke. "And gee, if it's slobbering over Solana you're concerned about, Tyler, I hate to tell you, pal, but for half the guys at this school it's too late."

Tyler glared at him, and their eyes locked. J.P. was deliberately baiting him. With J.P., *everything* was competition. And right now, he was trying to goad Tyler into a verbal battle. The problem with having J.P. for a friend was that J.P. didn't know *how* to be a friend. He only knew how to win.

Tyler had just opened his mouth to respond when Andrew said, "Hey, forget Solana. Jacie's the one I want."

"You know what, guys?" Tyler said, crumpling up his lunch sack—which of course he hadn't finished yet, "I know Jacie, and I know Solana, and I haven't heard anything from any one of you that comes even remotely close to—"

"Jacie?" Brian said. "Why Jacie? I mean, she's cute and everything—"

"She's stacked, man!" Andrew said. "Don't tell me you haven't noticed!"

"We've all noticed," Doug mumbled around his mouthful of hamburger.

"Yes, we have," J.P. agreed. "Definitely top-heavy. But I think our friend Tyler here is getting uncomfortable about our manner of speaking about his friends." Tyler had stood and was glaring not just at J.P. but at the rest of the guys around the table.

"Come on, Tyler," Doug scolded. "Knock it off. We're just talkin'."

"I know what you're doin'," Tyler growled. "I also know that people have the bad habit of believing this stuff. You say it to make yourself look big to the rest of the jokers around the table, and it doesn't matter to them that it's not true. They—"

"Well, now, Tyler," J.P. said, guzzling the last of his Coke and tossing the empty into a trash can nearby, "Jacie *is* stacked. I mean, that's a scientific fact. And Solana does have a kind of a—"

"I'll tell you what Solana has," Tyler said, pointing at his friend. "And Jacie too. They have the right to some respect. They have the right not to have parts of their body talked about by a bunch of morons who don't actually have any personal experience with girls' bodies, but want to make the rest of the morons *think* they do. And they have—"

"Tyler, Tyler," Doug said. "Hey—it's us, remember? Your friends. Your friends who happen to know that you think about sex as much as any of the rest of us. All you're sayin' is, you don't want us talkin' about *your* friends that way. But come on—*every* guy, even Tyler Jennings, when he sees a sexy girl, thinks about sex!"

"You know what?" Tyler said, stepping away from the table. "If I hang around here I'm gonna lose my appetite real fast."

And he walked away, hearing Andrew as he did: "Okay, I'm taking bets. Does he eat lunch with three girls? Four? Or does he get really lucky..."

• • •

Tyler pulled up in front of the middle school, hoping Tyra would be standing somewhere close by waiting for him. Fat chance. Nowhere in sight. He shut off his engine but, since his battery was fairly new and in good shape, left his radio on. Sometimes when conditions were just right, he could pick up a Colorado Springs station that played a lot of good stuff, some new, some old, most of it from artists few people in Copper Ridge had ever heard of. Right now they were playing a song by Nick Drake—a songwriter Tyler admired. Drake had recorded for just a few years in the sixties before committing suicide. Tyler often thought of all the musicians who'd died by suicide or accidental drug overdoses, wondering how things would have been different if they'd been Christians. Would their depression and despair have—

And, speaking of the sixties, here came Tyra. Today, she was into the retro look. Hip-hugging bell-bottoms, tie-dye shirt. Even beads. It was a look Tyler liked in old Woodstock movies, but worn by modern kids it was so—well, so fake. So self-conscious. So junior high.

He watched her break away from her knot of girlfriends, shouting and laughing back at them, waving, and then swing toward his car. Why couldn't she ever *walk* anywhere like a normal person? If she wasn't dancing, she was—how to describe it? Her body had a life and grace of its own; it was half art and half animal, a cross between ballet and a high-strung Arabian mare.

Normally, Tyler enjoyed watching her physical energy and grace. On this particular day, she had to walk right through a group of guys. Some of them Tyler recognized, some not, but how could a girl like

Tyra walk through a group of hyper-hormoned middle-school guys and not be noticed? And she was obviously noticed. She smiled at them, all white teeth and big, happy eyes, and every guy in the group turned toward her. Some talked to her, but Tyler was too far away to hear. His hackles rose anyway; he didn't like the way they were looking at her. And he liked it even less when she'd waltzed her way through the middle of them and they continued staring after her—clearly studying the part of her anatomy that had the most swing to it.

Tyler felt his mouth twist into a sneer. He'd like to grab a couple of those twerps and . . .

Tyra swung open the car door and flounced into her seat. "Hi!" she grinned.

"What did those guys say?" Tyler asked, staring past her to the guys on the grass, who had lost interest and turned back to their conversation as soon as she'd entered the car.

"What guys?"

"What guys. The guys who were memorizing your every move from behind all the way across the grass and the sidewalk."

Tyra glanced back at them, then rearranged herself and huffed. "Tyler," she scolded. "You're sounding like a big brother."

"I *am* a big brother. And I didn't like the way those guys were looking at you."

Tyra threw her book bag into the backseat and began digging through her purse for something while Tyler watched the punks on the grass. Should he say something to Tyra? But what? Tyra had no idea how a guy's mind really worked—how could he make her understand?

Funny this coming up on the same day he'd had that argument with his basketball friends at lunch. It must mean something. He thought about how J.P. and Jason and the others had talked about Jacie and Solana. Yep. He really ought to try to talk to Tyra about this.

He turned down the volume on the radio. "I wasn't kidding," he tried. "Those guys really were checking you out."

She still hadn't found what she was looking for in her purse. "Right," she scoffed.

"Tyra, I'm serious. Those little chimps were taking mental snapshots of your rear end."

She looked up at him. "You're serious."

"I *said* I was serious."

An awkward smile slowly formed on her face. "Really?" She turned and looked out the window. "Which ones?"

"Which *ones?* Tyra, don't you care that they were . . . that they were mentally undressing—"

"Was the guy in the black jacket one of the guys who was—"

Tyler accelerated away from the curb fast enough that he threw her back against her seat.

"Whoa," she said. "I just wanted to know—"

"Tyra, listen to me, okay? This is a subject I know something about. The thing is, guys are just wired differently than girls on this whole clothes thing. What appeals to you for one reason, appeals to us for another. What you grab out of your closet because, I don't know, maybe you like the color, the guys at your school would like because . . . because, uh . . . what's so funny?"

She burst out laughing. "Oh, Tyler. You're so funny when you try to be serious."

"I'm not . . . I mean, this *is* . . ." Tyler felt his face getting red. *Okay, calm down, take a deep breath, start again.* "Come on, Tyra, be honest. You don't really want those guys looking at you like that. But when you dress—"

"Oh, so now it's the way I dress? It has nothing to do with the guys now? It's my fault?"

"*No*, it's not—" Tyler stopped himself, thought, turned right on Buena Vista. "Well, yeah, maybe. Partly."

He could sense Tyra studying him, then shaking her head and turning back to the purse in her lap. "I don't even want to hear it," she muttered.

"I'd still like to break their necks," he said, reaching into the bin beneath the radio and rummaging around for a stick of gum. "But let's face it—if you'd been wearing baggy clothes when you walked through the monkey house back there, none of them would have given you a second look."

Her head snapped up. "They wouldn't have given me a second *look? Is that what you said?*"

"I meant—"

"So it's only my *clothes* boys notice? Gee, fashion conscious, aren't they?"

"I wasn't saying—"

"But it's too bad they don't find me just a little eensy-teensy bit attractive, isn't it? So that they might even notice my hair, or my face—"

"My point—"

"But no, it's my *clothes*—"

"Your *tight* clothes. That's my point. If you're going to wear tight clothes, or skimpy clothes, then you'd better get used to the idea that all those baboons are *not* going to be looking at your face, *or* your hair; they're just going to be looking at your bod. That's the way they—"

"No, that's what *you* would do, or your crummy friends. Did it ever occur to you that maybe all guys aren't—"

"But all guys *are*, little sis. That's what I'm trying to say. We're built that way. Maybe it's a holdover from caveman days, I don't know. We just—hey. What are you doing?"

Tyra had stuffed her fingers into her ears and begun to hum. He tried to pull one hand away from her head, but she twisted stubbornly away from him and hummed louder.

"Hey," he said, pulling up to a red light. "This is at least halfway important, what I'm saying here."

"I don't want to he-e-ar it!" she sang. "I'm *not* hearing it!"

"Well, you need to. I think—"

She cranked up the music volume—*way* up. Then she leaned over against the window, back turned toward him, fingers still in her ears.

Tyler looked at her, shaking his head. A horn sounded behind him, and he glanced up at the green light, then accelerated through the intersection. Then he looked back at Tyra.

Fingers in ears, back turned, singing—no, shouting—along with Dave Matthews.

Real mature.

Yeah, this was definitely something he was going to have to talk over with Mom.

chapter

Tyler wasn't much of a Keanu Reeves fan, and this movie sure wasn't going to change his mind. The guy couldn't deliver a line to save his life. But there weren't many theaters in town, and Tyler and Jessica had had their choice of this, the new Disney flick, and something where Shirley MacLaine dies a long, slow death from cancer.

Frankly, even if it had been a good movie, Tyler would have been distracted. In the dim light from the screen, he could see Jessica's left hand lying still on her leg. Her right hand she held up near her chest, as if she were playing with her necklace, but her left, the one nearest him, had been lying on that leg for some time now, tempting him.

Physical affection—holding hands, arms around each other, even kisses—had been easy between them when they'd dated last year, before she'd moved away. But since she'd returned, Tyler hadn't been sure whether that level of affection would be welcomed, so—afraid of rejection—he hadn't tried it. But tonight, she had seemed at ease and happy to be out with him. And there lay that hand. He'd been watching it for the past half hour, thinking about it, getting up his nerve, wondering what the risks were, what messages he would be sending her . . .

And then, he went for it. With practiced casualness, he reached down, gently clasped her hand, and lifted it to rest with his on the armrest between them. She turned and looked at him, smiled, squeezed his hand, and tucked her shoulder closer to him, a familiar move that, along with the soft warmth of the skin of her hand, brought back a landslide of memories.

From then on, Tyler only pretended to be watching the movie. He couldn't have told whether it was a comedy or a horror flick. He was aware of her thumb caressing the tender skin between his thumb and index finger, and of the artful way, tiny bit by tiny bit, the two of them each slipped a little lower in their chairs, a little closer together, till their shoulders snuggled cozily together and their heads were slight inches apart, and of the way her right hand slipped over to cover their two clasped hands. So easy, so natural. He relaxed into it.

There was, however, an odd thought that kept slipping into his consciousness. If—just supposing, hypothetically—Tyler were able to go out with Hannah, without her dad slipping a cog: Would they be holding hands like this? Snuggling? Aware of each other's physical presence as powerfully as Tyler was of Jessica's right now? Duh—not likely. Hannah would have jerked her hand away, embarrassed. Not that there was anything wrong with holding hands, but still, she would have, he knew it.

And that led him to an even stranger, even more troubling thought. Who would he rather be out with: Jessica, because she was a knockout and knew how to dress and let him touch her and touched him back sweetly and made him feel great? Or Hannah, whose faith and character he had to admit to himself he admired more, even if there would be no touching?

● ● ●

An hour later, Tyler smiled in anticipation as the middle-aged Hispanic waitress at José's set his combination plate down in front of him—two pork tamales, two enchiladas, and a taco, along with Spanish rice and frijoles. He inhaled the steam—*ahhh!* This was his favorite restaurant, and their tamales were the best things on the menu.

Jessica took a dainty bite of her taco salad. "Good?" she asked.

"Mmm-hmm," he mumbled, mouth full of steaming hot, wonderfully seasoned tamale. Mama Luz, Solana's mom, made the best tamales in the world. But José's were a close second—even better than some of the great Mexican restaurants he'd been to in southern California with his relatives.

Jessica seemed content just to watch him eat for a minute or two, then said, "Okay, tell me the truth—you really didn't like the movie, did you?"

He pointed to his mouth, finished chewing, and swallowed. Then he shook his head. "You know me. I'm an old movie freak. Give me Brando in *On the Waterfront* or Bogart in just about anything. And you have to admit, by those standards, Keanu Reeves—well. You know." He downed a forkful of beans and rice, then said, "Now—I answered your question. Are you going to answer mine?"

She looked puzzled. "Yours? You asked a question?"

"Yeah. Just before we got out of the car, I said, 'Why do you want to go to José's?' You don't even like Mexican. You never wanted to come here last year. And why did you insist that the waitress seat us in this big booth, rather than at a table for two?"

She dabbed at her mouth with her napkin. "First, a question for you. If you ever *did* get a bunch of guys together to form a band, would you still have time for me? You're so busy already, with basketball practice and everything."

A very odd question, Tyler thought. First, their relationship, if they were going to have one, hadn't been defined yet. Who knew how much time they were going to be spending together anyway, band or no band? And second . . . "It ain't gonna happen, so don't worry," he said, then popped another bite of enchilada in his mouth and talked around it. "The band, that is. I've already asked all the musicians I know."

She played with her napkin, smiling coyly. She hadn't eaten even half of her salad.

"*What?*" he asked.

"Maybe I know some musicians you don't."

"Oh yeah? Like who?"

Smiling widely now, she reached across the table and grabbed his hand. "I talked to that bass player I know. And he knew a drummer and lead guitarist who were free. So the three of them are coming here. Tonight. To talk to you about your band!"

She was so excited, so happy—Tyler couldn't tell her that the emotion surging through him as her words sank in was pure, unadulterated terror. He was going to have to talk to those musicians here? Tonight? But what if they knew a lot more about music than he did? What if they were a lot better? Why would they want to be in a band with him? And why, if they were good, experienced musicians, would they let him be band leader and lead singer? What if they didn't like him, and he had to watch his dream slip away one more time?

"That's why we had to come here," she explained, still smiling broadly. "And why we needed a big booth. See?"

He nodded, preoccupied. "You rascal."

"Look!" she said, pointing. Three guys were slouching in. Three tall guys with attitude—that was Tyler's first impression. Then he registered that all three of them looked familiar. The tallest one—

And then Tyler recognized him. Wade Anderson. Of course. When Jessica had said that she knew a bass player, Tyler should have realized that she was talking about Wade. When Jessica had been a freshman and Wade a senior, they'd created a minor sensation on campus by dating for a few months. Wade had been the campus rebel then, and after graduation, he'd started turning up in various local bands. Tyler had to admit that he was a pretty decent bass player.

Jessica waved, and the three sauntered toward their table. Tyler got up, came around the booth, and slid in next to Jessica, leaving the opposite side free for the three guys. He'd be darned if he was going to watch Wade sit next to Jessica on *his* date.

The guys all shook hands as Jessica introduced them. The one with his black hair in a ponytail and an earring in his left ear was Antonio Navarez, the lead guitarist, and the red-haired, freckled one Tyler recognized from school—another junior, Pat Johnson, a drummer. With some relief, Tyler remembered seeing Pat at a couple of Christian youth events in the past year.

"So you're thinkin' about puttin' together a band," Wade mumbled, motioning the waitress over.

Here goes, Tyler thought, not at all sure what one says to guys one is trying to sign up for one's band. "Thinking about it," Tyler said. "I write some stuff, play a little guitar, but I'm no lead player." He looked at Antonio. "You play mostly electric or acoustic?"

"Grew up on electric," Antonio said. "I was a big Hendrix fan. Clapton too; used to just listen to the stereo and copy their licks. But I play more acoustic now." He smiled. "Just like Clapton. Gettin' more into jazz now, crossover stuff. I like Pat Metheny a lot."

Tyler nodded, although the truth was, even though he recognized Metheny's name, he wasn't sure he'd ever heard any of the guitarist's music. "I play acoustic—but it's got a pickup on it in case we need it."

"Ever been in a band before?" Wade asked.

Tyler shook his head. "Just solo." He didn't bother telling them that he rarely performed even solo. "But my stuff needs a band. Do we need to talk about how much we'll need to practice, who chooses the music, when we—"

Wade held up a hand. "Too soon, man. Here's how it works. We all get together and play for a couple hours. If the music clicks, *then* we talk through all that stuff. If the music doesn't work, then no point in wasting time on talk. The music says it all."

● ● ●

"Do you think it'll work out?" Jessica asked as they walked slowly toward her doorstep that night, arms around each other.

"We'll see," Tyler said. "Old boyfriend Wade—" He pinched her side playfully. "Old boyfriend Wade was right about one thing—the music says it all. A week from today, we play together and find out."

"Excited?" she asked.

He feigned a yawn. "Who, me? Naaaah." They laughed. She stepped up onto her doorstep and turned around, now only a couple of inches shorter than he was. She set her hands on his shoulders.

"Now when you guys are famous," she smiled, "with your own private jet and adoring fans all over the world, don't forget little ol' me—who got you together in the first place."

"I won't. I'll have my secretary send you a card every Christmas." She shook a finger at him, mock-scolding.

"Thanks," he said quietly, looking into her eyes. He put his arms around her waist. "I wouldn't have thought of Wade. So you're right—none of this would be happening if it weren't for you."

She was quiet, her eyes huge, clear, bright. The light from the streetlight reflected in her hair. "For you, anything," she whispered, and tilted her head.

He continued to watch her, entranced, for several heartbeats before he realized that that was an invitation. He leaned forward and kissed her gently on the lips. They held the kiss, but not long, and he pulled back an inch and looked at her again. Her eyes were closed, the lids beautiful, translucent and glowing in the soft light. Then she opened them slowly, gazed at him, and they leaned into another kiss, this time longer and sweeter, promising more to come. Then she nuzzled her face into his neck, and he squeezed her tighter against him, wanting nothing else, wanting to be nowhere else in life than right here, right now. *How can I resist this? And why would I want to?*

● ● ●

We'll give Him all the glory . . .
We'll give Him all the glory,
Christ, the Lord.

Tyler turned his attention from the worship team in front of the congregation to Jacie, standing beside him, and a sudden memory came of when Jacie had actually been taller than him, along about fifth grade or so. Now she barely came up to his shoulder, and he could look almost directly down on top of her head. She didn't come to his church often; she attended a different one. But every now and then she seemed to want to share the worship experience with him. And he was always glad when she did.

For He alone is worthy,

For He alone is worthy . . .

Tyler often daydreamed through the sermon. He wasn't a note taker, and he had a hard time keeping his attention on the pastor during the 20-minute sermon. But during the worship part of the service, Tyler was tuned in. Always.

For He alone is worthy . . .

The four singers each had a microphone in one hand, and one hand lifted in that familiar posture of worship. Tyler was a little envious of that—he really wanted to have the freedom to raise his hands in worship if the mood struck him, or close his eyes, head raised, expression joyous and focused, as he sometimes saw others do. But he was too self-conscious for that. On those rare occasions when he tried it, he was conscious not of the God he worshipped, but rather of Tyler with his hands raised.

Christ, the Lord.

The tempo of the music picked up, and the heavyset woman on the right began a bouncing, dancing movement, clapping her free hand against the wrist of the hand that held the mike. Tyler liked her joy, her freedom.

He is exalted, the Lord is exalted on high,
I will praise him . . .

He was aware of Jacie's eyes on him, and he looked down, caught her grin—this was her favorite worship song—and smiled back at her. Then he gave her a double raised eyebrow, Groucho Marx style, and she rolled her eyes and looked away.

Tyler's mom and Tyra were sitting up near the front, on the other side of the sanctuary. Usually, Tyra sat with her friends, but today she seemed especially chummy with their mom; they were standing close together, their arms touching. And that was good. Tyler knew that his mom had a growing fear of the day—which she kept insisting wouldn't be long—when Tyler and Tyra would both be off at college somewhere. That would leave Mom home with nobody but Dad to keep her company. Tyler snorted and shook his head. Great company he would be—gone more than he was home, and when he was home, about as much fun as a grizzly bear with a toothache.

Jacie looked up when Tyler snorted, her expression curious. He shrugged. *Later*, he mouthed silently. She nodded.

It always surprised Tyler a little—and, truthfully, made him a little uncomfortable—that Jacie was so "tuned in" to him. He couldn't say or even think anything that indicated worry or uneasiness when he was around her, because she always picked up on it—always. No secrets. And maybe that's how the Brio team was supposed to be, but it still spooked him. Like she was inside his head or something.

The sermon was even less interesting than normal, and Tyler made time pass by going over, in his mind, the route he and J.P. and Richard would take that afternoon on their mountain bike ride. After considering lots of possibilities, he decided on a route that would give him a chance to explore a section of trail he hadn't tried before. But it would be a long ride, so when the sound of the organ swelled in majestic chords for the closing hymn, Tyler closed his Bible and stood, anxious to get an early start.

He maneuvered through the crowd like he was on a mission, shaking a quick hand here and there when he had to but finding ways to avoid getting drawn into conversations. Jacie stuck right behind him, and when they finally broke out into the parking lot, she said, "Hey—where's the fire?"

He turned and walked backwards as he answered, without slowing down. "Goin' mountain bike riding this afternoon with Richard and J.P.—we need to get an early start."

Her disappointment was obvious. But then, Jacie seldom made much of an attempt to mask her feelings; her face had always been easy to read, ever since elementary school. "Oh. I was hoping we could maybe eat dinner together, either at your house or mine. My mom would love to have you over; she always likes it when you come by. I think she's got a crush on you."

"How about next week?" he said, still backpedaling. "I really can't today. Richard and J.P. are gonna be looking for me in a few minutes." Well, not exactly true. He was supposed to call when he got home so they'd know when to show up. But obviously, there wasn't time for a dinner in there anywhere.

"Don't forget," she said, still looking disappointed. "Oh, hey—I'm almost afraid to ask, but how'd it go with Jessica?"

Tyler was a little surprised at his sudden reluctance to answer that question. But this was Jacie. He had to say something. "Uh—it was good."

She waited a beat or two. "Oh. It was good. Well, that explains it."

"Yeah. Well, you know, we went to a crummy movie, ate at José's . . . usual stuff." He thought of leaving it at that, but he couldn't. "One big thing, though."

She watched him. "Don't leave me in suspense," she said quietly.

"She asked Wade Anderson to help me get a band together. He's already got a lead guitarist and a drummer lined up." Well, that was a bit of an exaggeration; nobody was really lined up yet, including

Wade. They had to try each other out first. But no reason to explain all that right now.

Jacie's response, though, wasn't exactly what Tyler had expected. No smile. Her brows squeezed together, and she looked off somewhere over his shoulder.

"What?" he said. "I wasn't aware this was bad news."

"Oh—no, Tyler, I think—well, I don't know what to think. I'm sorry. I should be jumping up and down, but—Wade Anderson?"

"Yeah, Wade Anderson," Tyler said, feeling defensive.

"Is he—he's not a Christian, is he?"

"I'm not asking him to preach, I'm asking him to play bass. It's the lyrics of my songs that are Christian."

"Yeah, I know, but—oh, I'm sorry, Tyler, I'm reacting all wrong. You've wanted this for a long time, and I'm really happy for you."

"I hope so. You don't sound like it. But remember what you three were saying about Jessica the other night—about the two of us living in different worlds? Maybe that's not always such a bad thing, huh? That's how she came up with a band for me."

Then he watched Jacie shrink back in on herself, her eyes radiating hurt. *What did I say now?* he wondered. But frankly, right now he didn't even want to find out. "Listen, call me tonight and we'll talk about it some more. But right now I gotta jet. So—listen, I'll see you later. Okay? Okay."

Without waiting for her response—which would probably be something that would require another response from him anyway—he hopped into the car, fired up the engine, and headed out of the parking lot. A quick look in the rearview mirror before he pulled out onto the street showed Jacie still standing right where he'd left her, watching him leave.

chapter 9

Panting, wiping sweat from their eyes, Tyler, Richard, and J.P. straddled their bikes on a hogback ridge, scouting out the new trail that wound downhill among dry, rocky outcroppings and sparse trees on a fairly steep slope.

The ride over the first half of the trail, the familiar part, had been breakneck and too fast—just as the three of them liked it. But they had known the trail, and in most places could see far enough ahead to spot any hazards—any other cyclists coming the other direction, for instance, or a tree down across the trail. They'd been lucky; the trail was clear, and they'd had it all to themselves.

Richard munched a power bar. "So, how many people have died on this stretch here?"

J.P. snorted. "Only a hundred this month, and they were all wienies. Personally, I could do it backwards, blindfolded."

Richard nodded. "The backwards part I can understand, just in case you meet any chicks. You won't scare 'em away with your face. But the blindfolded part has me puzzled. If you're going backwards, why be blindfolded?"

"So I won't have to look at you, since you're gonna be so far behind me," J.P. said, standing on the pedals and balancing.

"Except," Tyler said, "if you were riding backwards, and he was so far behind you, he'd really be way ahead of you, wouldn't he? And you wouldn't be able to see him, blindfolded or not, unless you had eyes in the back of your head, in which case you'd need two blindfolds, right?"

"Ha-ha," J.P. said. "Joke about this." And he launched himself down the hill.

"Sounds like he had no ready comeback for the blindfold crack," Richard observed. "But he'll be tough to beat on this hill."

"Yeah, J.P. has a great sense of humor—except when he's the butt of the joke," Tyler agreed. "But what he lacks in sophistication, he makes up for in speed. Speaking of which—eat my dust." And Tyler, who had to admit to himself that eating dust was just what *he* was doing, except in this case it was J.P.'s dust, shot down the trail as fast as he could with reasonable safety. Or at least with the amount of safety the three of them considered reasonable, which meant it would have scared the fat out of anyone sane. And it very nearly scared the fat out of Tyler, too, because he'd never even scouted this part of the trail before and had little idea of what was ahead. But J.P. seemed to have survived so far, judging from the occasional glimpses of him Tyler caught speeding between rocks and tree trunks. So the trail was apparently navigable, even if it was frighteningly steep. He wanted to check on Richard, but he was afraid to turn around, and afraid to slow down lest Richard run into him. So he had no choice but to press ahead as fast as he could, and look for a way to pass J.P.

Fifteen minutes later, nearing the bottom of the hill and, Tyler assumed, getting fairly near the trailhead again, there it was. The trail had cut back to the left, and J.P. had followed it. But if Tyler left the trail and simply maneuvered down an outcropping of bedrock that looked fairly passable, steep but mostly smooth and even, he could pick up the trail again *ahead* of J.P. Unless J.P. was indeed riding backwards, in which case Tyler would end up behind him again. But Tyler couldn't spare the brain power to work through that; he needed to concentrate on staying in one piece.

Which turned out to be harder than Tyler had expected. Picking his way down the bedrock, he noticed that, gradually, the slope increased. Tyler went from pedaling to coasting and, too soon, to riding his brakes to keep from losing control down the steepening slope. No wonder the trail had cut back—whoever had blazed that trail, deer or coyote or mountain biker, had just been avoiding suicide.

Okay, Tyler told himself, *no problem. I've been on worse slopes. Sometime. I must have been. Sure. Key is just to keep my speed down, keep my weight back, avoid mistakes . . .*

After Tyler passed a wide-limbed, windswept spruce on his left, he was tempted to look back over his shoulder to check on J.P.'s progress. But he couldn't do that without taking his eyes off the rock surface ahead, which didn't seem like a sane thing to do. So Tyler kept his eyes ahead, wondering if Richard had been stupid enough to follow him down this slope. Not likely. Richard was relatively sane.

Just a little farther—the trail must be right past that yawning crevice up ahead, where all those bleached human skeletons and rusting hulks of mountain bikes commemorate the boneheaded decisions of past generations of—

The problem was that he had let his speed climb a tad too high, so that when he cut left to avoid the pit ahead, he lost his balance, had to correct his turn a fraction to the right to regain it, and suddenly his front wheel fell away beneath him. He was aware of falling, of some kind of bone-jarring impact, of pain, of somebody grunting like a pig as all the air was forced out of his lungs . . .

● ● ●

"Splash a little more water on his face."

"No way. We got to save what's left for when he wakes up."

"What if he doesn't wake up? One of us has to ride back to town and get an ambulance or a medevac chopper or something."

"I think he's waking up."

"Uh-uh. He's out, man. Look at him."

"I'm lookin', meathead. Look at his eyelids. They're flickerin'. Kind of."

"They are not. He's stone-cold out."

"He is not. Look."

"He is too."

"I am not," Tyler said.

"Yes you are."

"I am *not*. I heard everything you said."

"Oh, yeah? What did I say about you and Jessica?"

Tyler struggled up on his elbows. "Ouch!" And then sank back onto the ground. "Man. What happened?"

"Well, you racked up your bike," J.P. observed.

"Oh, *man!*"

"I think it's rideable," Richard said. "Really. It did get scraped up and dinged a bit, but I don't think any moving parts are bent, except a couple of spokes, and we can just pull those out and you can replace 'em next week."

Tyler reached up and J.P. took his hand and lifted him to his feet. "Ah!" Tyler winced when he tried to put weight on his right leg. "Ow. *That's* a bit tender. So—where was I when I fell?" He looked around.

Richard pointed up the hill. "Actually, you were almost down to the trail again. You lost it right there," he said, pointing, "only bounced a time or two, and then plopped on your back right here on the trail."

"You lose," J.P. jeered.

"Well, technically," Richard pointed out, "Tyler did get to this point on the trail before you. So he was ahead when the race was called on account of injury. Which means—we have a winner!" He reached up to high-five Tyler, who winced when he tried to raise his arm that high and gave up.

"I think not," J.P. sneered. "And anyway, he wasn't on his bike when he hit the trail, so he's disqualified."

"All that proves," Tyler coughed, "is that I can beat you *without* a bike. Flat on my back. Unconscious."

"Ha!" J.P. said. "So you *admit* you were out cold."

Richard and Tyler looked at each other.

A moment passed.

Richard raised an eyebrow.

"I'd have an answer to that," Tyler said at last, "if my brains weren't splattered all over the rocks here." He scuffed with his toe the wet spot on the trail where he'd fallen.

"That's where we splashed water on your face," J.P. said. "If it was your brains, it'd be a much smaller spot. And anyway, the injury time-out is over, so the race is back on." He wheeled his bike around, threw himself into the saddle, and disappeared down the trail.

Tyler sat on a rock beside the trail, trying to clear his head. He was suddenly aware of all the sensations he'd been unaware of while concentrating on the race: the squawking of magpies in the pines and spruce and Douglas fir trees around him, the wind cooling the dusty sweat that ran down his face and sides, the clamminess of his sweat-dampened shirt, and how incredibly thirsty he was. His hydration pack was still on, but he had to reach around and search, his bruised muscles protesting, to find the drinking tube that had been pushed awry. The water was cold and sweet.

"You were only out a minute or two," Richard said.

"Ha. I wasn't out at all. I was fine."

"Uh-huh. Right."

There was gritty, itchy dirt everywhere—in his hair, inside his clothes, in his ears, even in his mouth. He looked around. "How can it be such a beautiful, sunny day in a mountain paradise, and I feel like I got dropped out of a space shuttle from three miles high?"

He tested his right leg. Not sprained, he didn't think. Maybe just bruised a little. Should still be okay for basketball the next day. He twisted his torso, tested his arms. His left forearm was sore; he twisted it to see a good-sized raspberry below his elbow. "Well, that'll look good for a few days."

Richard chuckled. "You were lucky, man. You bounced down that hill like you were in a pinball machine. Lucky your head ain't broke."

"My head was already broke before I left the trail, or I wouldn't have."

"No, really—"

"Hey!" J.P.'s voice drifted back up from lower in the canyon. "This is the trailhead right here! I can see the road!"

Tyler looked up at Richard, shook his head briskly, then stood and picked up his bike, looking it over. He grimaced, even though the damage was minor. He loved this bike.

● ● ●

"All right—*what* did you say about me and Jessica?" Tyler asked five minutes later, as the three of them glided down the rough-but-paved canyon road, Richard on one side of Tyler, J.P. on the other.

"Hey—why ask?" J.P. responded. "You already heard it. You weren't out—right?"

"Yeah, I heard it, but there was a magpie squawking in my ear as you were talking, so . . . come on. What?" Tyler's right leg was sore enough that he let it rest on the pedal and pushed only with his left.

J.P. grinned and rode silently for a few seconds, stretching the tension. Then: "Obviously, you *were* out, or you'd know I didn't say *any*thing." J.P. cast a victorious glance at Tyler and held it for a few yards, savoring the moment. "But there is one thing I want to know about Jessica," he continued. "Same old question, man. Are you stakin' a claim? 'Cause that's cool if you are. You were there first. I just want to know, that's all."

There was a pause, then Richard said, "Is he asking what I think he's asking?"

"Hey, it wasn't you I was asking, Casanova," J.P. said. "So let the man answer."

"I don't care if you were asking me or not," Richard said. "What is it with guys like you, that you automatically assume every girl in school is interested in going out with—"

"Come on, this is the same lecture I got from Tyler *last* Sunday. Let up already, you two. It's not like I knock girls over the head and drag 'em off by their hair. But if she's interested—"

"What you do isn't that much better, J.P.," Richard snorted. "You take 'em out a few times, get what you can out of 'em by makin' 'em fall in love with you, and then—"

"Hey, that is *not*—"

"The heck it isn't! And Jessica is too classy an act to fall for it anyway, so forget it. She'd see through you so fast you'd never—"

"Too classy an act? Listen to this guy. Hey, Tyler, maybe I'm not your competition."

"Ladies, ladies, please," Tyler said calmly. But as he spoke, he studied Richard, riding beside him. And Richard, clearly upset and embarrassed, would not look back.

Ah.

"So Tyler—you got an answer? What's it gonna be?"

Tyler kept his eyes on Richard a while longer, thinking. Then he looked slowly back at J.P. as the three of them rounded a turn onto Leadville Avenue. "I hear you." *Ouch.* Sharp pain in his right knee. He straightened that leg and coasted, taking advantage of the slight downhill slope.

J.P. shook his head. "No, you already heard me, days ago. Now I want to hear you."

"Not yet."

"Yes yet." J.P. stood and sped up, calling back over his shoulder, "I want to know by Friday, Tyler, good buddy—or else I make your mind up for you!" And he accelerated around another corner and out of sight.

The two of them pedaled along silently for a while, the late afternoon sunshine painting the mountainsides around them a golden red. Snow covered the higher peaks, and Tyler shivered slightly as the wind from those peaks carried the feel of ice down to him. He stole a glance at Richard every now and then, but Richard wouldn't look back.

It was Richard who spoke first. "You ever wonder why we put up with J.P.?"

The question surprised Tyler. "Do you?"

"Yeah, I do."

"Well, let's start with the fact that we've all been friends since elementary school."

"Great, fine. But even then he was an arrogant little snot. You know what gets to me now? It's his utter lack of respect for anybody. Except maybe you, Tyler. But anybody else—and especially girls! He just uses 'em and throws 'em away. Disposable. Like plastic spoons or something."

"Plastic spoons?"

"Best I could do on the spur of the moment."

Tyler thought for a minute. "Two things. First, you're absolutely right about J.P. And yes, it bugs me big time. But I'm not going to stop being his friend because of it. Becca once told me that if J.P. wasn't responding to my witnessing to him, I should give up and stop spending time with him at all. But I think she was wrong. I think my friendship with him *is* part of my witness to him. And if I dropped him just because he wasn't responding, then I was being dishonest— my friendship wasn't really a friendship at all, it was just a way of manipulating him. Does that make sense?"

Richard looked at him oddly. "I don't know. I'll have to think about it."

"Second thing—this whole discussion about J.P. is your way of avoiding the thing about Jessica. You want to talk about it?"

Richard snorted. "What's to talk about? No, I don't."

"I didn't know you felt that way about—"

"You still don't. I haven't said a word. J.P. can think whatever he wants. He's off base about everything else, so why not this?"

"But if there was—"

"Tyler, we've had this conversation before. You and J.P. can pretty much get any girls you want to go out with you, and then there's guys like me who can't. Period. End of discussion. Believe me, Tyler, guys like me learn that it doesn't make any difference which Mercedes you like if you can't afford one."

A few more minutes of silence. Then Richard cleared his throat and said, "Listen, uh—Tyler? The photo shoot last weekend, all that talk about Jessica and Hannah—"

"Ow!" Tyler interrupted. "Man, my leg's gettin' worse. Let's slow down a bit."

They slowed. Tyler waited, but Richard didn't continue his thought. When they stopped for the light at Buena Vista, Tyler said, "Go on. Something about the photo shoot."

Richard shrugged. "No, it really wasn't about that. I just—well, which one *are* you going to choose?"

The light changed, and Tyler pedaled on for a couple of blocks before he tried to respond. "Richard, man, I don't even know how to answer. I mean, in the first place, you know Hannah doesn't date, right? And I don't just mean she won't go out, I mean she won't have a boyfriend. They don't believe in it."

"I know that," Richard said. "So you're going to choose Jessica then?"

"You know what, Richard—it's not about choosing one or the other anymore. That's sort of how I thought it was last weekend, at the photo shoot, but—but then I had this talk with Hannah. I mean, what am I supposed to do about Hannah?" Now his right leg was stiffening up. He'd be hobbling for a day or two. "The thing about Hannah is, I've never met anybody like that before. I mean, I've known sweet girls before, like Jacie, but Hannah has this . . . this goodness."

Richard shrugged. "Yeah. And it doesn't hurt that she's tall and blonde and looks like a magazine cover."

Tyler shook his head. "No. I mean, yeah, she does, and yeah, that's probably the first thing I noticed, but . . ." He laughed. "But you know what? I'm done talking about this, because I don't have the slightest idea what I'm talking about. And on a related subject—" He swerved slowly closer to Richard and put his hand on his shoulder as the two rode side by side. "Believe it or not, I found some guys who are interested in starting a band. If we set up a practice, you want—"

"Oh, my gosh!" Richard exclaimed, looking at his clunky sports watch that had every possible function on it including, probably, a two-way Dick Tracy videophone. "Look at the time. My mom's going to kill me! It's way past time to feed the goldfish!" He accelerated away. "Listen, it's been great, Tyler—see you tomorrow. Let's do this again!"

AllenOlson: Imagine finding a nice kid like you in a place like this. Especially this late. What's up?

ColoradoTy: nothin. worse than nothin. doin research for a paper. you?

AllenOlson: Just checking email. Anything interesting going on in your life?

ColoradoTy: feelin a little banged up. went mountain bike ridin with jp and richard up rock creek this afternoon, took a tumble. no big deal. somethin bothers me about that trip, though. was listenin to richard and all of a sudden it hit me—he likes jessica. you know, as in romance, as in the L word. duh—not sure why i never noticed it before. now that i realize it, it's been right there ever since she got back—he likes her and figures he doesn't stand a chance, so he just lets it go. so i feel kind of guilty about it, you know? because i could have her and i'm not sure i want her, and he wants her and couldn't have her if he tried. or something like that.

AllenOlson: Ego, ego, O great one. Thou givest thyself too much credit. The fair Jessica, unless I misseth my guess, is not under thine thumb quite yet. In fact, it wouldst not surprise me if the fair lady herself be not the one whose thumb is the stronger. She hast wiles thou knowest not of, killer. And I admit I hath not known thine friend Richard well, but underestimate not the appeal his kind of heartfelt, feckless, sincere social klutziness hath for dewy maids. They often dig the geeks.

ColoradoTy: feckless? i said that once and got my mouth washed out with soap.

AllenOlson: Anyway, I judge from your comment about not knowing if you want Jessica that you're still between the horns of a dilemma, as it were. Is it not so?

ColoradoTy: you been readin ``increase your word power'' in reader's digest again? and don't even ask about the girl situation; i'm tired of everybody thinking they have some right to demand answers about that. although i must say jessica has earned some points these past couple of days. i'm truly touched. you know how i'm always sayin i'd like to form a band but can't find anybody who wants to join? she went out and found me some guys.

AllenOlson: I'm speechless. Tell me about it.

ColoradoTy: long story, and i type slow, so i'll just say she knew how important it was to me, and she knew some guys who play, so she got us together to talk it over. we hit it off and now we got a practice comin up saturday in my garage.

AllenOlson: Wow. This is incredible. I'm happy for you, I really am. These guys Christians?

ColoradoTy: one or two i'm pretty sure aren't. others, maybe. i'll find out. i thought about that a lot and what i'm thinkin is, this could be a chance to share the gospel. they hear my music, what it's about, and maybe they'll want to know more.

AllenOlson: Yeah, very good point. I was wondering about two things, though. One, are they going to be interested in playing a steady diet of Christian music? Because that's what you write. And I assume you're thinking of this as a band that will play your music. And two, how are they going to feel about playing in church? I know you'll want to perform at some church activities. Right?

ColoradoTy: hey, i already had this lecture from jacie. we haven't even gotten together to practice yet. so hold your horses, cowboy. when we see if we want to keep playin together, we'll hash that stuff out. i just wanted to tell you jessica came through for me, which i definitely think is a point in her favor. and yeah, i'm excited about getting a band together.

AllenOlson: Me too. Really. I mean, I know you've wanted this for a long time. And I hope it works out for you, I really do. But let me ask you this: now that you're this close, how are you going to feel if it doesn't work out?

ColoradoTy: hey, sunshine. i tell you something cool and you throw water all over it.

AllenOlson: Whoops. Sorry. But do you hear what I'm saying? I've been listening to you play for a few years now, Ty, and you have a unique style, a unique approach to rhythm and song structure. (That's what happens when you have a musician for a wife—you notice stuff like that.) What if those things, that idiosyncratic approach to music of yours, just doesn't translate well into a band context?

ColoradoTy: idio—what? drop that thesaurus this minute. besides, i thought you were gonna stop.

AllenOlson: You're right. Sorry. Hey, really, Ty, I'm happy for you. And I really hope it works out just the way you want it to.

ColoradoTy: i can tell.

AllenOlson: One last question, nothing to do with the band—do you and Jacie ever date?

ColoradoTy: me and jacie? jacie? wake up, old man. it was jessica we were talking about.

AllenOlson: No, I know. It's just—I mean, she's attractive, she's your friend already, which is a good start, she's a believer—what, do I have to draw you a picture here?

ColoradoTy: maybe you better. i'm not trackin. jacie's one of the brio chicks, man. my buds. that would be, like—very weird.

AllenOlson: You used to date her a few years ago, am I right?

ColoradoTy: no, wrong again, mr. wizard. we were like little kids, seventh grade or something. we couldn't even drive. we thought holding hands was a big sexy deal. you call that dating?

AllenOlson: Okay, okay, pardon my stupidity. It was just something I was wondering about.

ColoradoTy: sheesh. i mean, that would be like dating my sister. or something. jacie? sheesh.

chapter 10

Tyler struggled against his sheets for a moment, groggy, lost, con-fused—then slowly realized where he was, and why he was awake in the middle of the night. He felt the speed of his beating heart, heard in his ears his own rapid breathing, and knew exactly why.

He'd had a dream.

Half of him desperately wanted to get right back into it. And the other half was appalled at himself for having the dream in the first place.

Because the dream had been about Hannah. Pure, sweet, innocent Hannah.

And it had been a steamy, pulse-pounding, guilty—well, R-rated dream.

Tyler sat up in bed, wiped his damp face with his sheet, and searched the shadows around his room. Only in the past couple of weeks had it gotten so chilly that he'd stopped leaving his window open through the night; he much preferred to sleep with fresh air and wake up chilly in the morning. But now the window was closed, the curtains limp. The room felt stuffy, too hot.

He fumbled blindly at the messy nightstand beside his bed, trying to find the glass of water he usually kept there, but all he managed to do was knock a book and a few other things off, creating a clatter in the still night.

Shapeless shadows formed on the walls, the floor; the only thing he could identify in the gloom was his guitar.

Tyler rubbed his eyes, then his forehead. What a dream. What a— what a contradictory mix of feelings. He tried to figure out why. There was no point in denying it; he was—and had been since the first day he'd met her—aware of Hannah in a very physical way: of her face, of her long, lean body. She was . . . well, she was, even though the thought would no doubt horrify her, a very sexy girl. In a very different way from Jessica, of course, but very sexy anyway. If she'd been more cynical, more worldly, less moral, less Christian, she would be exactly the kind of girl J.P. would love to take out and see how far he could get. She had the looks.

Was that why Tyler felt so ashamed of his dream? Because he wanted to be different from J.P.? Because he thought he was connecting with Hannah at a deeper level than J.P. ever could with any of his conquests? Because he wanted to have a relationship with Hannah that honored God? And because his dream had just shown him that, in truth, he wasn't any better than J.P.?

Or was he ashamed that half of him—at least half—wanted nothing more this minute than to fall back asleep and slip right back into that dream?

He arched his back, stretched, yawned, shook his head, settled back down into his waterbed, pulled up the sheets, twisted and tossed till he found a halfway comfortable position.

But just as he did, he also found a very *un*comfortable question: If the dream had been about Jessica, instead of Hannah, would he have felt guilty at all?

He doubted it.

And did that tell him something about Jessica—or about himself?

Hurrying back to his car that afternoon, running late after a long basketball practice, Tyler saw a girl sitting by herself on the steps of the science building, her arms propped on her knees and her face buried in them. Distracted by thoughts of a heavy load of homework, he didn't pay much attention—until she lifted her face to wipe the tears from her cheeks, and he saw that it was Hannah.

He stopped, stood a moment, unsure what to do, then jogged to where she sat. "You okay, Hannah?"

She glanced up at him and then looked away, apparently embarrassed. Then she waved toward the bike rack nearby. "My bike," she said in a broken voice.

He scanned the bike rack till he spotted her beat-up, older ten-speed touring bike—without its front wheel. "Uh—something's missing."

Hannah pressed her face into her hands.

For the first time, Tyler wished he was one of the "cowboys" on campus who carried bandannas. One would come in handy right now. "Hey, uh, listen, I'll go get you a tissue or something." He ran into the science building and found the closest men's room. In the stall, he whipped several yards of toilet tissue off the roll, then ran back to Hannah and handed it to her.

She wiped her face with it, blew her nose—then looked at what he'd given her.

"Sorry—best I could find," Tyler apologized.

She grinned a lopsided grin at him, then her face twisted again and she held the tissue against her face. "I locked it up," she protested. "I thought it was safe. I thought . . ."

"Well, the thing is," Tyler said, sitting on the step beside her, "most bikes these days come with quick-release hubs on front and rear. Which is great if you're working on your bike, putting on new spokes or something—they're very quick. But that also means you have to lock it up with the chain through both wheels, or some guy who needs a new front wheel just comes along, whips that thing off in about a second, throws it in the back of his—"

"Tyler," she said, "I know all that. I always lock it through both wheels. This morning—I don't know, maybe I was in a hurry or something, or had something on my mind—" She stopped, looked up. "That was it. I had a test first period I was worried about. I guess I wasn't paying attention." She sighed, then wiped her cheeks again.

A moment's silence; Tyler watched her. "How long have you been sitting here?" he asked.

She shrugged. "I don't know. Oh, Tyler, I feel so—so violated. No one has ever stolen from me before."

"Wow," Tyler said, shaking his head. "You *have* been sheltered."

She sighed again. "I should call home. Somebody will have to come get me. Can I borrow 50 cents? I don't even have any change to call with."

"Hannah," Tyler said. "It's all right—everything will work out. And I'm *glad* you don't have 50 cents." He reached into his pocket. "That gives me the chance to come to your rescue, to be your knight—" A sudden thought occurred to him. "Hey. Skip the 50 cents. Let's just load your bike, or what's left of it, in the trunk of my limousine and I'll run you home in style."

She looked up sharply, a little shocked. "Oh—thanks, Tyler, but I can't."

"Why not? It won't be like we went on a date or something. It's late, your bike won't work, you need to get home—I doubt your parents will be upset. They'll probably thank me."

"But we'll be alone in the car, just the two of us—"

"We're alone right now, sitting here on these steps, and you're not worried about that. A car is practically a public place. You can't pull the drapes or something—you're sitting there where everybody can see you."

Hannah looked over at her bike. New tears welled in her eyes. "I feel horrible. Now my dad will have to buy a new wheel, and we don't have a lot of money to spare. And all because I was careless."

"People make mistakes, Hannah," Tyler said. "I think your dad will understand."

She looked at him as if he just didn't get it, but she said nothing.

"Hey, you don't have to be so down on yourself."

Hannah sighed, staring at the deformed bike.

Tyler stuck out his hand. "Key."

Hannah put her key ring in his hand.

He unlocked her bike, wound the chain around the seat post, and picked it up. "Come, fair maid. Your knight in shining armor has a limo right around the corner."

Five minutes later, with her bike filling up the Escort's floor just behind the front seats, Tyler pulled his car out of the parking lot. Hannah seemed stiff, quiet, uneasy, and it occurred to Tyler that she had probably never been alone in a car with a boy before. *I'm her first,* Tyler thought.

Hannah sat silently for several blocks—as did Tyler, since he really couldn't think of anything to say, now that he actually had her to himself, alone, in a way he never had before. *What's the matter with me?* he wondered. *I usually talk too much—and now I can't even come up with a comment about the weather.*

"So I bet it's a lot colder up here than it is where you come from, right?" Tyler said. "This time of year, I mean." He was glad no one else was in the car to witness his humiliation.

Hannah looked strangely at him, then said, "No, actually, Michigan is a lot further north. Most of the time I think your weather here is pretty mild."

Tyler nodded. "Hmmm."

If somebody made a tape recording of this conversation, Tyler realized, *I would pay a lot of money in blackmail to keep it from ever becoming public.*

And then, there it was—his salvation. He flipped on his blinker, braked abruptly (throwing Hannah against her seatbelt suddenly enough that he heard her gasp), and turned into the Dairy Freez parking lot. "Okay, don't get weirded out or anything," he said, "but I want to buy you a Coke and some fries."

"Tyler!" Hannah said, sounding frightened. "This is *not* a date!"

"No! No, I know," he reassured her. "Everything's cool. We're not doing anything wrong here. We both know what's going on." He pulled into the drive-thru lane. "Your bike broke down, I'm just giving you a ride home, etcetera, etcetera. Okay? But—since you're feeling rotten about getting your front wheel ripped off and all that, I'm doing my Christian duty to try to cheer you up. Now if you just happen to sit here sipping your Coke and *pretending* to be on a date with the most magnificent, sought-after guy in the entire junior class, well, who would even know? Right? Chance of a lifetime to walk on the wild side."

Hannah actually grabbed the door handle. "There's a phone over there. Maybe I should—"

"Whoa, whoa. Forget the 'wild side' comment—I must have lost my head there or something. Really, I just want to buy you a Coke. I *am* trying to make you feel better. Let me do this one small thing for the cause of better relations between our peoples, hmmm?"

Hannah's uneasy expression eased somewhat. "I think we come from the same 'people,' Tyler."

His eyes widened. "Really? Gee, I thought with the obvious basic cultural differences, the language barrier—"

She swatted his arm lightly. "Tyler." But the tension had been eased, and he began to feel like himself again.

Three minutes later, the girl at the drive-thru window handed him a couple of Cokes and a bag with two orders of fries and some ketchup. But instead of pulling back onto the street, Tyler pulled into a parking spot and cut the engine. Hannah looked at him questioningly—but not, at least, with suspicion this time. He pointed to the fries. "Can't drive and eat my fries with ketchup at the same time, or at least I haven't figured out a way yet. And I didn't figure that you'd want to be seen feeding me as we drive around town." He ripped open a ketchup pack.

She shook her head. "I don't want to be—no offense—seen driving around with you at all, Tyler. You don't realize. If somebody from our church sees me with you in the car, drinking a Coke, and tells my dad—"

"I'll tell you what. If you get in trouble over this, how about if I sit down with your dad and explain the whole thing? I mean—come on—I *know* he wouldn't want you sitting there in front of the school all night."

"No." She sat with eyes locked on her food, eating slowly. "No, he wouldn't."

"All right then." They were silent for a moment, munching, and then Tyler said, "Now, if this *were* a date . . ."

"Tyler!"

He laughed. "Teasing!" But she didn't laugh back. He watched her out of the corner of his eye for a minute or two, and then something struck him. "Shoot, I'm sorry. I'm fooling around like nothing's wrong, and you're still worried about your bike, aren't you?"

She nodded. "How will I get to school tomorrow?" And as soon as she'd said that, she raised a warning hand. "And no, don't even bother offering—I'm not riding to school with you. Besides . . ." Her voice trailed off, but her hands still moved as if searching for words. "How can I make you understand? My dad makes a decent salary, but he has passed up a lot of opportunities to make more because he has his priorities straight. And my mom has never worked away from home; she's been too busy with her number-one job. So we're a one-income family. And all of us are expected to help cope with that. Which means getting by with less than other kids, and making our clothes last longer, not asking for anything we don't really need—"

"And making sure you take good care of your stuff so it doesn't get ripped off," Tyler finished for her.

She nodded. "And now I have to go back home and tell him I didn't keep up my end of the bargain."

"And you're afraid he'll be angry."

She looked up. "He might be, but it's more likely that he'll be hurt. He'll feel like I've let him down, that he trusted me with something important and I proved that I couldn't be trusted. And I'm supposed to be a good example to my brothers and sisters. I'm supposed to be the responsible one they look up to."

"And you *are* someone they can look up to, Hannah. You're a great example to them."

Hannah shook her head. "No, I've let them down. I've let them all down. Not just *them*, but I've also let God down."

Tyler knew that his surprise was showing on his face. "Let *God* down? Are you serious? I mean, I let God down all the time, but it has nothing to do with my bike, or my car. Hannah, think about it. *You* didn't rip off somebody's bike wheel. Somebody ripped *yours* off. *That* was the sin here. You were the victim! So stop beating yourself up already."

She looked out the window. "I disagree. You don't seem to understand what I'm trying to say."

He waited till she turned back toward him, then nodded. "You're right, I don't. There's a difference between a sin and a mistake. Isn't there? If you catch your sleeve on a nail and rip it, you may have ruined your shirt, but it was a *mistake*, not a sin."

"Not being careful is a sin," Hannah argued. "Not taking proper care of your possessions is a sin. Letting your parents down is a sin—that's the same as not honoring them. So it's not as simple as saying—"

"Wait a minute. Who says those things are sins?"

She looked at him as if he came from another planet. "The Bible, Tyler."

"Where?"

" 'Honor your father and mother.' It's one of the Ten Commandments, plus Jesus said it at least twice in Matthew—"

"I know, I know. But are you saying that forgetting to string your bike chain through your front wheel, because you were worrying about your test, was failing to honor your parents?"

"Yes. Of course."

He struggled to understand. "Wow. I mean—wow. Hey—let me

make a guess here. The reason you were worried so much about that test in the first place was that if you didn't do well on it, you wouldn't be honoring your parents. Right?"

She looked at her lap, smiling a little. "Right."

He laughed a little. "Hannah, you are like really, *really* hard on yourself, you know that? Will your parents really get angry with you?"

"No. But I know I've let them down."

"Where do you get these ideas then, Hannah?"

"I take my standards from the Bible, Tyler. As every Christian should. You sound like they were *my* rules. And they are, but I didn't make them up. I just accept what the Bible says."

"Yeah, but . . ."

"There are no 'buts' in the Christian life, Tyler. No compromises."

He sipped his Coke, watching the cars rush by on the street. "I know what you're saying, but my friend Allen always says to remember that the Christian life is more than a set of rules, and that the worst thing we can do as Christians is let ourselves get burdened down with guilt that Christ already died to take away."

"Tyler—" Hannah started to respond, then lapsed into silence. Tyler waited for her to continue, but when she did, it was just to say, "There's no more fries."

Tyler looked at the bag on her lap. "Sure there are—you have some. Plenty," he said.

She smiled and pointed toward his empty bag. "No, yours. There goes our excuse."

It warmed Tyler's heart to hear her describe it as "our" excuse. He grinned, then said, "Well, you could give me some of yours. Then I'd still have some."

She shook her head. "When I talk to my dad about what happened, I have to be honest with him, Tyler. And your fries are gone."

He started the car. "Yes, honesty is good." But as he pulled out onto the street again and began driving slowly down the road—as slowly as he felt he could get away with, actually, to prolong this unexpected and precious visit—he realized that he'd have been willing to be a lot less honest.

And maybe he still was, if it came to that. This time with Hannah was something he had wanted for weeks now, and it was almost over. What could he do, what could he say, to make it last? What small thing could he take away from this conversation to make him feel that he hadn't completely blown the opportunity?

"Turn right at the next stop sign," she said.

"I know."

She looked back at him. "How? You've never been to my house."

He shook his head. "Remember, I grew up around here. When I first met you and you told me where you lived, I knew exactly which house."

She smiled. "Yeah, if we were back in Niles, I guess I could have done the same."

He turned onto a road lined with ponderosa pines and only a few other houses, then checked his speedometer and cut his speed a couple of miles per hour. "Small town? You knew everybody?" he asked.

She shook her head. "It wasn't really that small."

"You had lots of friends back in Miles?"

She shot him a give-me-a-break look. "Niles, Tyler. Niles. And the truth is, I didn't have a lot of friends there. Remember, I was home-schooled. I had two close girlfriends most of the time I was growing up, both from my church."

Tyler cut his speed a little more. "I know you didn't date or anything, but—was there some guy you liked? Some guy that, you know, if you *did* date, and if—"

"No, not really," she interrupted. "Nobody like that. The only guys my age I knew were at my church, just a few of them. And they were all so immature."

"So, now you're *surrounded* by guys your own age—"

"And they're all so immature," she said, and they both laughed.

"Snips and snails and puppy dog tails," Tyler said. "I admit it. But, uh—" Would she answer this? "Isn't there now, maybe, some guy you've met since you've been here that, uh—"

"Here's my driveway. Turn—oh, Tyler, oh no! My dad's home early from work. Look—he's standing out front, waiting!" She looked at her watch and gasped. "I'm an hour late. I had no idea it was so late. I should have paid more attention and called to let Mom know what happened. What was I *thinking?*"

Tyler pulled into the long dirt driveway and stopped in front of the old farmhouse-style home. Hannah jumped out. "Oh, Daddy, I'm so sorry I didn't call! I was so upset because the front wheel of my bike was stolen, and Tyler offered to drive me home—Tyler, this is my daddy; Daddy, this is Tyler Jennings—and I didn't realize how late it was . . ." Her voice trailed off, and she looked like a five-year-old.

Tyler got out more slowly, then opened the back door of the Escort and lifted out the one-wheeled bicycle. As he did, he watched Hannah's father—who, despite the sober look on his face, touched Hannah's shoulder gently, lovingly, as if to reassure himself that his daughter was all right. "I was worried, Hannah," he said, his voice deep. "I wish you had called to let us know. I was just about to go out looking for you." He looked up and met Tyler's gaze. "Thank you for bringing my daughter home." He wrapped an arm protectively around Hannah's shoulders, as if to leave no doubt whose she was.

And Hannah, Tyler noticed, seemed safe there. At home. She sent him a minor apology with her eyes, not speaking. And as Tyler stood nervously for a moment or two longer, in silence, he realized that her father wasn't going to say anything else.

"Well," Tyler said. "Guess that does it, then. Hope you find another wheel for your bike." He opened his car door, then looked back once more at Hannah and her father.

And then, without warning, a scene flashed into his mind from his dream of the night before—a scene with wild eyes and hard breathing—and Tyler felt his face grow suddenly hot. Hannah looked at him strangely, as if she could see that something had happened to him, but he looked away, unable to meet her clear, innocent eyes. Tyler felt, rather than saw, her father's eyes studying him. "Uh—bye then," Tyler said. He hurried into his car, started the engine, and backed out of the driveway.

But he hadn't even gotten back to the stop sign before he was slapping himself on the forehead, yelling, "Aaahh! What's *wrong* with me!" He'd had at least a half hour with Hannah. A half hour to find out how she was feeling about him, to find out something important about her, to collect some precious thought or word from her to take home and cherish. And he'd *blown* it. He had nothing—nothing, that is, except the memory of her father's searching gaze as Tyler had stood before him, as nervous and unsure of himself as a little boy.

He pictured, in his mind, the protective way Mr. Connor had held her lovingly and tightly against his side. He pictured the way Hannah had relaxed against him. Safe at home.

And what had Tyler been doing? Replaying scenes from last night's sexy dream.

He's right to protect her, Tyler thought miserably, accelerating back into Copper Ridge as quickly as possible. *From people like me.*

chapter 11

Tyler was settling into bed with his newest copy of *Guitar Player* magazine that night, planning to read for a half hour or so before going to sleep, when someone knocked at his closed bedroom door.

"Abandon hope, all ye who enter here," he called.

His mom opened the door, smiling. "I always do." She was dressed in her thick, purple terrycloth robe, her funky flannel pj's underneath. She looked, as Tyler always thought, very pretty. She looked so young that no one ever believed she had a son his age. Most of his guy friends seemed to either dislike or barely tolerate their parents, but Tyler admired everything about his mother.

She sat on the edge of his bed. "You mind?"

"Well," he said, "I was about to read this article on Marilyn Manson, but I can give you 10 seconds first."

She pushed soft, loose curls out of her eyes. "Right. Marilyn Manson. Just your style."

"Okay, Dave Matthews then."

She nodded. "That's closer. Speaking of music, is everything ready for your band rehearsal this weekend?"

He closed the magazine. "Well, I wouldn't quite call it a rehearsal. It isn't even a band yet—we're just trying each other out. But yeah, it's all set—as soon as I clean out the garage. Since Dad's not here, if you're still planning to be gone Saturday..."

She laughed. "Yes. You don't have to worry about being embarrassed by your parents. I won't be running out with trays of lemonade and cookies."

He lay back. "Too bad. We could probably use some. Well, I'll just have the groupies bring some out."

"In your dreams. Hey—been writing any songs lately?"

"I sang you that one I wrote last month. I've been working on a couple more."

"I'd like to hear them."

"Not ready yet."

She nodded. "Well, when they are. I always like to hear your music."

"Now there's an unbiased opinion if I ever heard one."

"Nobody said I had to be unbiased," she smiled. "And when you've got a son as wonderful as I have, it would be pretty hard anyway."

They looked at each other quietly for a moment, and Tyler could feel that his smile matched hers. Both he and Tyra had gotten her looks—for which he was grateful. The last person he would want to look like was his dad. "You came in to ask about Jessica, didn't you?" he said.

She raised one eyebrow, amused. "He's not only talented but psychic, too."

"You know," he said, mildly protesting, "I told you I'd keep you informed. You don't have to pry."

"Not prying," she said. "Just giving you an opportunity to keep me informed. Without even getting out of bed, no less. What service." When he didn't say anything right away, she went on, "I thought—well, you've gone out with her a couple of times now, and I thought maybe you could tell me how it's going."

Tyler fought the inclination to tell her nothing, then realized that, actually, he wanted to hear her thoughts. So he explained to her, much as he had to Allen Olson—but without mentioning the kiss on Jessica's doorstep—the different ways that Hannah and Jessica made him feel, and his confused attraction to both of them. He even told her what Allen had said.

She listened very carefully, studying his face, his eyes, his expression, and Tyler knew that she was hearing and weighing every word. When he finished, she nodded and was quiet for a moment. Then she said, "I want you to promise me something."

"Something *else?*"

She laughed. "Something different this time. I know that Hannah doesn't date. I know that she's not going to be your girlfriend. Still, I want you to promise me that you'll never lead either of these girls on as if they were the only girl you were interested in. It's very important—*very* important—that they both know that you're not seeing just one girl exclusively. *Even Hannah* needs to know that you're not *interested* only in her." She smiled. "Girls who don't date still have hearts that fall in love."

Tyler's heart leaped at the thought, but he kept his words more subdued. "Do you really think she—"

His mom chuckled. "Tyler, I don't know. But I do know this: Girls feel these things differently from guys. A teenage girl may not give her heart more easily than a teenage boy does—I think *all* teenagers give their hearts way too easily—but girls give them more completely than boys do. Let's say Jessica thinks she has won you, not realizing that you're still as attracted to Hannah as you are to her. She'll probably let herself fall head over heels in love with you, 100 percent. And then if she finds out later that she wasn't your first choice—one broken heart. And girls remember those broken hearts all their lives."

Tyler studied her, thinking. "Since you don't really like Jessica all that much, why do you want to make sure she doesn't get hurt?"

She reached, touched his forehead lightly. "This isn't about Jessica, Tyler. Or even Hannah, as much as I like her. This is about you. What kind of man you're going to be." She watched him carefully, and he knew she was making sure that he was tuned in, that he was hearing her. "A lot of men, Tyler, a lot of smart men, concentrate on finding the right girl. And that's a smart thing to do. Very important. But a *wise* man concentrates on something else. He tries hard to be the right man."

They sat without talking, looking into each other's eyes, as that sank in. And Tyler knew that they were both thinking exactly the same thing. The *right* man would work hard to make a good home, a place where everyone was supported, loved, at peace. The *right* man would be more concerned about doing his job in the family well than he would be about criticizing the job done by others.

Unlike his dad.

Then she smiled. "There's something I like very much about what you're saying tonight, Tyler. I think that you are asking all the right questions. And if you ask the right questions, I think you'll find the right answers. When it comes to romance, some men only think with their . . . hormones. I like the fact that you're actually trying to figure all this out rather than just acting on your hormones."

He leaned a little closer and whispered conspiratorially, "So tell me—what are those right answers?"

She smiled and leaned until their foreheads were touching, their eyes an inch apart. "I can't tell you. It doesn't work that way."

Tyler straightened up and laughed. "You're kidding! This is a mom's golden opportunity! Her son is asking her to explain how the whole love and romance thing works, and she says no?"

She chuckled, then let her gaze sweep across the room. "Oh, I guess I'd love to choose your girlfriends for you, Tyler. But no parent can do that. Hannah or Jessica—the truth is, parents often don't see all there is to see in our children's friends. We see in them certain things we're looking for, but the danger is great that we'll miss many other things. And besides, there are some lessons you only learn by slogging through them. And I think this is one of them." She patted his arm. "Thanks for telling me all this. I knew you would handle it well, Ty. But sometimes a mom just has to hear it." She sat for a moment, looking at him. "Anything you want to talk about?"

Actually, there was. But . . . "Nah," he said. "I guess not."

She tilted her head. "You almost said something. What was it?"

"No, it's okay."

"Now's a good time. Might as well spill it."

He lay back on his pillow, looking up at the ceiling. "Well. I was listening to the guys talking about girls the other day, what they notice about them, how they like them to dress, all that stuff. They were even talking about Solana." He glanced at his mom, wondering how she would react.

"Ah," she said.

"That was bad enough. But then I started thinking about how Tyra is . . . well . . ."

"She's growing up," she finished for him.

"Yes. I mean, she dresses real cute and everything, but . . ."

Mom nodded. "She may only be 13, but sometimes she looks like she could be 16 or 17, doesn't she?"

"Tell me about it. And don't you think she dresses in a way that shows off her body too much? Mom, I don't *want* those guys—or the junior-high version of those guys—talking about my sister the way they talk about Solana or somebody. You know what I mean?"

She sighed. "Tyler, this time I know exactly what you mean." She wrapped her hands around one of her knees, pulled it up, and rocked a bit on the bed. Tyler waited, knowing she was thinking this through before answering. "There is no greater minefield for a teenage girl," she said finally, "than fashion. You probably think teenage girls dress the way they do to attract guys, right?"

"Well—*some* do," Tyler said.

She nodded. "Some do. But most of the time, and for most girls, that's not it. Teenage girls base their sense of fashion on what *they like* or what *other girls like*, not on what guys like. Most of the time, they dress so that their circle of female friends will like their clothes. That's what Tyra is doing, Tyler. She dresses in clothes *she* thinks are cute, but it's the approval of her girlfriends she's seeking."

"I was saying kind of that same thing to the guys the other day. But then they started talking about Solana. And you can't say that Solana dresses like she does to impress Jacie and Becca." He had almost used Jessica as an example and was glad he'd caught himself.

His mom shrugged. "Probably not. Most girls do notice how guys respond to certain kinds of dress. Some girls use that to attract and gain power over guys. Solana does exactly that. And I worry about that in her. But the other girls, like Becca and Jacie, dress in what feels comfortable or makes them feel good about themselves. Tyler—" She turned back toward him and smiled. "Mom is on the job. Tyra and I talk about these things, and believe me, I watch like a hawk to see what she wears. If I ever catch her starting to dress like Solana, she'll wake up one morning and find that her entire wardrobe has been replaced with nuns' habits and combat boots."

The two of them shared a quiet grin, imagining the dancing Tyra dressed like a nun.

"Sweet of you to worry about this, Tyler," she said. "And I know when you see Tyra, you see the little kid she's always been and think you need to protect her. But just as I like the man you're becoming, I see the woman emerging in Tyra, and I like that woman I see. There will be tumultuous days ahead for us, I'm sure, but she will emerge on the other side of that chaos a woman you and I will both be proud of."

"Your crystal ball tells you so?" Tyler asked, tossing his magazine onto the floor and scooching down into his waterbed.

"Madame Jennings knows all," his mom whispered, and kissed his forehead.

chapter 12

Tyler was climbing a stepladder Saturday morning to lift some boxes onto a high shelf in the garage when he heard, even above the blast of his boom box, a metallic clatter. He slid the boxes into a free spot on the shelves and turned and sat on top of the stepladder, grinning. "Hey, ladies," he called. Solana, Jacie, and Becca, bundled in sweatshirts, knit caps, and jackets, sat astride their bikes in the open garage door. Becca tossed down the wrench she'd been using to whap the empty gas can on the floor beside her.

"Could you turn that music up a bit, please, Tyler?" Solana shouted.

Tyler hopped down from the ladder and turned the volume down.

"I don't know about you, Tyler," Becca said. "Still listening to Dylan . . ."

"If you're interested in songwriting," Tyler said, "who better to listen to than Bob Dylan?"

"Yeah, but he's . . . I don't know . . . I mean, my *dad* listens to Dylan."

Tyler shrugged. Someday, he would sit the girls down and make them listen to one of the Christian albums Dylan had recorded back in the seventies. But he didn't have time for that today; he had too much to do. He grabbed a plastic garbage sack and started scooping up stray trash from the floor and stuffing it in.

"I hope your parents are paying you well for this, Tyler," Solana said.

"Not paying me at all. I've got a band practice here this afternoon."

"Oh, yeah, the famous band."

"Yeah. Which I already told you about, including the practice in my garage today. So why are you asking?"

"Well," Jacie said, stepping off her bike and leaning it against the side of the garage, "we're just hinting around to see if you're polite enough to ask us to help, or whether we have to pitch in without being asked."

With his back to the three of them as he continued filling his garbage bag, he grinned. "You came over here to help me clean the garage? No ulterior motives?"

"We figured you'd be so grateful you'd take a bike ride with us up Rock Canyon," Becca said.

Tyler shook his head. "Sounds like fun, but I don't have time. I've gotta—"

"You'll have time if we help," Becca said. "Won't he, girls?"

Solana let her old bike drop on the ground. "Point us in the right direction."

With the four of them working hard, the job was done in 20 minutes, and Tyler brought out four cans of soda.

"You guys are life savers," Tyler said, popping the top and gulping the ice-cold Dr Pepper.

"And that's why you owe us a bike ride," Jacie said.

Tyler lowered his can and burped loudly.

"Gross!" Becca said.

Solana burped even louder.

"Will you two stop it!"

"Can't," Tyler said.

"Can't stop it?"

"That too, but what I meant was I can't go on a bike ride. Gotta run through my songs to get ready."

"You have to practice for your practice?"

Tyler laughed. "Yeah. I do. I have to pick the songs I want to try out with—"

"Know what, Tyler?" Becca interrupted. "We just saved you an hour or more of work, and it's not even 11 o'clock on a Saturday morning, and you've got puh-lenty of time for a bike ride before you sit down with your guitar."

"Right," Jacie said.

"Right," Solana said, starting to lift Tyler's mountain bike down from its ceiling hooks.

"Whoa! Hey!" Tyler said, reaching to stop her. "You'll drop it."

"Get it down yourself, then, big guy, or else I will—and yeah, maybe I'll drop it and smash it beyond repair."

Tyler set his Dr Pepper on the floor and lifted the bike down. "I want to be back here by noon. Everybody got that? I really do need to practice."

Within a minute they were on their way toward Rock Canyon. Tyler tilted his head back, closed his eyes, let the cold, clean mountain air rush past his face, through his hair. He was glad, actually, that the girls had come. Glad for the help in the garage, and glad for the chance to relax on a bike ride this morning. And glad for their presence, despite their teasing and bossiness.

He opened his eyes and studied the mountains in the morning sun. There were few clouds in the sky, and the pines and fir were dark green in the sunlight. A Clark's nutcracker swooped low over their heads with one loud squawk.

The girls, their bikes clustered together five or six feet in front of him, had been chattering for a while, but he hadn't been paying attention to what they said—till he heard the name "Hannah."

" . . . asked her out," Becca said.

"She was real sweet, though," Jacie said. "Just calmly explained that she doesn't date, didn't try to make him feel bad or anything."

"Who?" Tyler said. "Who asked her out?"

"Hey, look who's back from the dead," Becca called back to him. "Mention Hannah, and suddenly he wakes up."

"Ha. Who?"

"Ha who? What are you, an owl?"

"Who asked Hannah out?"

"Only about half the guys in school," Solana said, drifting back to ride next to him, "at least until they figure out she doesn't date. But recently, Greg James. Unless we count you kidnapping her in your car on Tuesday. Come on, 'fess up—did you steal the bike wheel yourself so you could give her a ride home?"

"Oh," Tyler said, relaxing back onto his saddle. Greg James. Chubby guy who didn't look like he shaved yet. Probably wasn't even as tall as Hannah. "How do you know he did? She tell you?"

"Of course," Becca said grandly. "She tells us everything."

"Mm-hmm," Tyler said.

"Including everything about you, of course," Becca added.

There was quiet for about half a minute, broken only by the occasional murmur of the creek. Then Tyler said: "What, uh—what did she say—"

The three girls suddenly whooped with laughter. "Oh, Tyler," Solana said, barely able to speak. "You're too much. Just have to find out how she feels about you, don't you?"

Tyler felt his face getting hot. "That's not what I was trying to do."

"Yeah, right," Solana said.

Another minute or so of silence. He and Solana sped up to join the others so that they all rode four abreast up the canyon road, their breath coming in white puffs of vapor. Then: "She didn't tell you anyway," Tyler said.

No one answered.

"You don't know," he scoffed, then waited. But still no reply.

He tried again: "*I* know, but you don't kn—"

Again, the three of them erupted in laughter. "Tyler, Tyler. No, you *don't* know," Becca said, "and it's driving you crazy. She's so transparent, and yet so hard to read, because you've never met anyone like her. What's a boy to do?"

"Now, if he wants to know how *Jessica* feels . . ." Solana said.

"Yes, not nearly as hard to figure her out," Jacie said.

"Tell you what," Tyler said. "Before we get started on Jessica, I need to know where we are on the whole Jessica thing."

"What do you mean?" Becca asked.

"You know. We had that Alyeria talk last week, then the thing at the mall—the whole 'two different worlds' discussion. I just need to know if we're all okay about that. I just keep getting this feeling . . ."

"What feeling?" Jacie asked.

"Well, like I'm being pulled again. You know. Between you guys on one side and Jessica on the other. Like last year. And that's what I said I *wasn't* going to let happen. So what's up?"

A short pause. "Nothing," Becca said at last. "Everything's fine." Silence.

"Well—then why isn't anybody talking?" Tyler asked.

"Tyler, *mi amigo*," Solana said. "Ask yourself something. Since Jessica got back, how much time have you spent with her, or talking on the phone with her? Now ask yourself how much time you've spent with us. And how much time *would* you have spent with us if Jessica weren't around? So . . . yeah, we're feeling a little deprived."

"And that's why you came over and helped me clean my garage?" Tyler asked, feeling defensive. "Because you wanted to rag on me about—"

"*No*, Tyler," Jacie said, hurt. "We came because we wanted to spend time with you."

Becca chimed in: "She comes back and suddenly you guys are all the time together again. Too bad Hannah *doesn't* date. Believe me, you'd be better off with her. Jessica's—"

"Becca, you just don't like her, plain and simple. You think she's—"

"No, that's not it! Really. I'm *trying* to like her, even trying to be her friend. Did I tell you that Tuesday, while you were kidnapping Hannah, Jessica and I had a nice, long talk?"

Tyler was surprised. "No." He and Jessica had talked twice since then, and she hadn't said anything about it.

"Well, we did. And, of course, being me, one of the things I talked about was my faith, about how important God is to me, and about how my life is changing . . ."

Tyler had a sinking feeling.

"And, Tyler, all I can say, is—it was like, *whew!*" Becca swiped her hand once above her head. "Right past her. Didn't connect at all. It wasn't like she was rejecting it—it was like she didn't *get* it. Tyler, this is a girl who doesn't have a spiritual dimension to her. At least not yet. There's just—I don't know. Something missing there."

Tyler drifted back behind the others and rode in silence, thinking of Hannah's comment about Jessica a few days before: *But when I talk to her about spiritual things she kind of skims right by it. I think that, even if I believed in dating, I wouldn't want you to date Jessica.* And all he had heard in that was the possibility that, just maybe, *Hannah* would like to date him. He hadn't been listening.

What would Allen Olson say about this conversation? Whose side would he be on? Tyler's or the Brio girls'?

He remembered Allen's challenge: *Imagine that you have married Jessica. Ten years from now, what will her influence upon your life have made you? Deeper, stronger, closer to God, a man of integrity and character? More materialistic, less interested in spiritual things, more sensual? Then project yourself ten years into the future with Hannah as your wife. How has she influenced you?*

Maybe he hadn't been listening to Allen either.

"Tyler? You still with us?" Jacie asked.

"Yeah," he said.

"We *are* trying with Jessica. You need to know that."

"But it's a little hard," Solana added, "with someone who belongs on the cast of *Friends.*"

"Solana!" Jacie scolded.

Becca slowed until she was riding beside him. "I know you didn't want to hear what I said a minute ago," she said. "And you probably feel like we're ganging up on you or something. But Tyler, listen. Tyler, buddy? Brother? One of my oldest and dearest friends? Kissy kissy make up love love love? You hearing me?"

"*I'm* not kissing him!" Solana said.

When Tyler looked across at Becca, who had moved her bike very close to his, he saw the tender and gentle look that he had often seen on her face—but not as often, he suddenly realized, since Jessica had arrived. "Hey, look, it's Becca," he said. "Where you been for the past couple weeks?"

She smiled. "Here's the point. We just want to walk with you through this. To help you think things through. It's like a puzzle. You can point out the things we're missing about Jessica. Yeah, we're a little jealous of her, it's true. And maybe that blinds us to some things. You can tell us the things about her that we've been ignoring but that you see clearly. That's *your* piece of the puzzle."

"My piece?"

"Yeah. And we've got pieces too. We see things about Jessica that you don't. And none of us will have the complete picture till we all share the pieces we have and put them together. That's all we're trying to do."

"Yeah, but some of your pieces sound unfair and harsh—"

"What did we say that was harsh?" Becca asked, surprised.

"Well," Jacie said, "the thing about belonging on the cast of *Friends* was a bit catty. Solana?"

"All right," Solana grumbled. "I apologize." Then, in a quieter voice, she added, "But it was true."

"We have an instinctive caution about her," Becca said. "An inner voice that's telling us that there are parts of her not developed enough yet to make her a good match for you. Tyler, you would drive each other crazy because of that, believe me. Please hear us. We love you. We want you to be happy. Maybe someday Jessica will be the woman who will make you happy. Someday. But not yet."

Tyler opened his mouth to speak, but Jacie said, "Tyler?"

He looked at her.

"Let's not talk about it any more today. Promise you'll think about what we said. All right?"

He pedaled on.

"Okay?" she pressed.

"Okay," he said.

It happened anyway, didn't it? he asked himself. *Here I am—torn between Jessica, who I really like, and my best friends.*

● ● ●

"Hi, Tyler!" Jessica's excited voice said when he picked up the phone after lunch. "All ready for this afternoon?"

"I think so," he said. "Good timing. I just finished running through my songs. I didn't want to play so much my fingers get sore."

"Makes sense. Tyler, I am so excited for you! It's going to go great!"

Well, on one side, he had a girl who knew it was going to go great, and on the other, three who just wanted him to be happy. How could he miss? So, in that case, why did hearing Jessica's voice keep reminding him of the things Solana, Jacie, and Becca had said a couple of hours before?

"I hope they left you enough time to practice," Jessica said.

"What? Who?"

"Your three friends. I was out driving around this morning and I saw the four of you on your bikes. I figured they'd dragged you off while you were still trying to get ready. Sometimes you have a hard time saying no to them."

Hmm. Something in her voice he wasn't sure he could identify. Not jealousy exactly. Possessiveness? He couldn't be sure, but whatever it was, it made him uneasy. "No, it was fine. Actually, they helped me get the garage cleaned out and ready for the guys. Saved me a lot of time—"

"Oh, Tyler! Why didn't you tell *me* you had to do that? I'd have been glad to help!"

Jessica helping to clean out a garage? Somehow he had a hard time picturing that. Did she even own clothes she could get dirty in? If so, he'd never seen them.

"Tyler," she continued, "I really hope . . . well . . . never mind."

"What?"

"Well, I hope the three of them weren't trying to come between you and me. You know. Saying things about me. That kind of thing. They want you all to themselves, and I'm a threat to them. And last year, they said a lot of things that—well—just weren't true."

Tyler rubbed his eyes. They *had* said some things about her this morning. But . . . "No," he said, "I really don't think they said anything like that. Maybe they've grown up a little since last year. I don't think they would say something that wasn't true, something that might hurt you. The truth is, I think they'd like to be your friend."

There was a short pause. Then: "Anyway," she said, "I'm so glad you're all ready. I really have a feeling about this afternoon. I've got my fingers crossed for you!"

Tyler knew she meant well—she really did. And she was the one who'd set up the whole thing, and he wouldn't forget that. But keeping her fingers crossed for him? The last thing Jacie and Becca had done for him this morning before they'd headed home for lunch was gather around him, put their hands on his shoulders, and pray about his band practice.

Yep. Two different worlds, all right.

chapter

"Where do you want us to set up?" Wade had backed his van into the driveway near the open garage door. Antonio jumped down from the passenger side and opened the tailgate, revealing instrument cases and amplifiers.

Tyler swept his arm toward the open area he and the girls had cleared in the garage that morning. "When Pat gets here, he can set up in the back, you guys right in front of him—"

"This is rehearsal, man," Antonio chuckled. "Not a performance. There's no audience. We got to see each other. Like in a circle or something."

"Antonio, you set up over there," Wade said, hauling a huge amplifier out of the back of the van. "I'll be next to you so I can keep an eye on your left hand."

Pat arrived and backed his little station wagon into the driveway.

"We can't play in the cold, man," Wade said, his breath puffs of vapor in front of his face. "You got some heat out here?"

"Yeah," Tyler answered, "some space heaters." It had been getting steadily colder all day, even though the sun was still high. He scooted the three electric space heaters he'd scrounged from all over the house closer to where the band would be playing, and cranked them all the way up. "They blow it out pretty good. I think we'll be okay. Wow," he said as Antonio opened his guitar case. "A Les Paul! An old one, too."

Antonio shook his head. "Not as old as it looks. Guy I bought it from just didn't treat it very well. It's a '79."

"Still . . ."

"What do you play?"

Self-consciously, Tyler gestured toward his guitar leaning against the wall. "Japanese Ovation knockoff. But the action's pretty good, and the pickup's decent."

To Tyler's relief, Antonio didn't seem contemptuous. "They amplify pretty well," he said. Then he looked around. "Where's your amp?"

"Uh—I didn't think I'd need one for practice."

Antonio shook his head. "You will if me and Wade are plugged in. Those Ovations don't have much volume. We'll never hear you." He nodded toward his own amp. "Plug into mine. I'll take the main. You take the auxiliary. Controls are on the right. Need a cord?"

"Uh—yeah."

Antonio tossed him one. "Used the pickup on your Ovation lately?"

"No, not in—uh, a year or two."

"Better change the battery. They drain quick in those little condenser pickups. Probably takes a nine volt."

Tyler jogged into the kitchen, frantically searched through the junk drawer for a battery, and then rushed back out into the garage. He loosened the strings, installed the new battery inside the guitar, then tightened his strings again. By that time, Pat had his drums set up and was playing a minute, making adjustments, playing a minute, making adjustments . . .

"We got everything in here now?" Tyler said. The other musicians nodded without looking up. Tyler pressed the garage door button, and the door closed.

Antonio and Wade were gathered around an electronic tuner. "Plug 'er in and tune 'er up, man," Wade said. "We're about ready to start."

Tyler plugged in his guitar, strummed—and breathed a sigh of relief when the sound of it actually came from the amp. He adjusted the volume, then checked his tuning. When he finished, Wade and Antonio were already working through a chord progression that sounded familiar to him, but he couldn't quite place it. Pat would play a few measures, adjust, play, adjust—Tyler wondered whether drummers always took this long to get set up.

"Come in any time, man," Wade called.

Tyler moved a couple of steps so he could see Antonio's left hand better, but the lead guitarist was using odd chord positions Tyler couldn't figure out. "Where are we?" he called after a minute of struggling.

"It's 'Tears in Heaven,' by Clapton," Antonio said. "In D."

Tyler concentrated, but it was no use; no way could he reproduce on his guitar what Antonio was doing on his, or even figure out which chords to strum.

"Try something else," Wade called, and launched into the familiar bass run of the Beatles' 'Lady Madonna.' Tyler nodded enthusiastically; familiar ground at last.

"Okay," Wade yelled when they'd gone through the verse a couple of times instrumentally. "Try the vocal!"

Try the vocal?

On a good day, Tyler would probably have been able to come up with about half the words to an old song like that. But like this, with Wade, Pat, and Antonio watching him, waiting? "I, uh—I don't know the words!" Tyler yelled. "Got 'em written down or anything?"

The other musicians slowly wound to a stop, with Antonio drifting off into a long, noodling run and Pat shifting rhythms, repeating a pattern that seemed to please him, and then—what a surprise—reaching over to adjust something.

"Listen," Wade said, with some impatience, "the thing is, we need to hear your voice, get a feel for how you handle a song. So why don't *you* choose one?"

Good idea. "Okay, let's play, uh . . ." The other three stared at him. Tyler laughed nervously. Silence stretched. "This is weird. I'm drawing a blank."

The three looked at each other, and then Antonio said, "Well, how about Dylan, then? Know any Dylan?"

God bless Bob Dylan. "Yeah, sure. How about, uh—'Maggie's Farm'? Or 'All Along the Watchtower'?"

"Hendrix version?" Antonio asked, launching into the power chord progression of Jimi Hendrix's "All Along the Watchtower."

"Nah, let's do 'Maggie,'" Wade said. "Better jam song. What key?"

"C!" Tyler shouted, and Pat and Wade immediately began laying down a strong rhythm, to which Antonio added a few licks. Tyler, grateful that the first line of the song was easy to remember, felt a surge of self-doubt when he realized that what he was playing didn't seem to match what the others were doing.

"Add a seventh!" Antonio called.

Add a what? Oh—a seventh chord? Tyler tried a C-seventh—and yes, there it was! He launched into the vocal, and although he seemed to be off by about a half measure and had to stall and stammer to get into the rhythm, he almost laughed when he realized how much easier the vocal was with that seventh note thrown into the chord.

Concentrating as he was on the vocal, on watching Antonio's left hand to keep up with the chords and choose the right ones, Tyler made it halfway through the song before he glanced at Wade and saw him grinning and looking behind Tyler. Tyler turned for a quick look—and there was Jessica, slipping in the side door. No wonder Wade was grinning—she looked outstanding: tight black jeans, hiking boots, heavy reddish turtleneck that, despite its thickness, still managed to leave no question about her figure. But at the moment she was smiling back at Wade, and Tyler felt a quick surge of jealousy—and forgot the words.

To cover, he pretended he was bailing out of the song to say hi to Jessica.

"Hey," he shouted, turning out of the circle of musicians and taking a step or two toward her. "Didn't know you were going to drop by."

"Wouldn't miss it," she said sweetly. "I knew you guys would be doing good music. That sounded great! Don't you have a mike for your voice, though?"

Tyler wasn't sure he *wanted* a mike for his voice—he felt too unsure of himself. But Wade, who had stopped playing, said, "Antonio, we still got those mikes in the van?" And before Tyler knew it, each of the four of them had a mike, connected to a mixer sitting on a box near Wade.

"Okay," Wade said, "let's try a couple of verses of 'Maggie's Farm' again to get a level."

They launched into the song, with Tyler putting a lot more into the vocal now that he had an audience. *I've got it, man,* he thought with exhilaration. *I've got a band! And we sound good!* He turned and grinned at Jessica, and she grinned back, nodding her head and dancing side to side with the music. *I can do this! I AM doing it!*

"Try some harmony!" Wade yelled. "Let me get a level on the other mikes!" Wade and Antonio moved seamlessly into strong, tight backup vocals. *Wow, these guys are good,* Tyler thought. *They've done this before.*

"Pat, come on—I need a level!" Wade shouted.

"I can't hear it—I can't find a line to come in on!" the drummer yelled back.

"Come in on top—high harmony!"

"I can't hear it!"

Wade rolled his eyes. "Then double up on the melody with Tyler!"

But the melody didn't work well with both of them singing it. Pat had a completely different approach to the delivery of the lines, and the two of them stumbled over each other.

After a couple of minutes of singing, with Wade setting the levels at the mixer, he nodded, turned back into his mike, and they finished out the song.

"Have you guys tried any of Tyler's songs yet?" Jessica asked.

"Let's stick with the tried and true," Wade said. "We still don't have the feel—"

"Well, wait," Antonio said. "We're not all playing from the same repertoire anyway. If he's got some lead sheets, that might work better."

Lead sheets? What was a lead sheet? "Uh—well, I don't have much written down. Just the lyrics with guitar chords written in."

There was a pause. "Whatever," Wade said resignedly.

"Hold on," Tyler said, unstrapping his guitar and hurrying toward the house. "Uh—hey, Jessica? Could you get everybody a drink? Sorry I didn't think of that before, guys. I've got soda in the fridge. Nobody's home but us. Dr Pepper, 7UP..." He bolted into the house.

This was it. He could feel the goose bumps breaking out on his arms and neck as he charged up the stairs. He was about to hear *his own songs* with a full band! Maybe they could even work up some background vocals...

But *why* hadn't he thought to gather up some lyric sheets for his songs ahead of time, even make up some new ones a bit more legible than the scrawled things he always sang from? Just because he could read his own chicken scratching didn't mean anybody else could. And where were they? Frantically, he swept through the clutter on his desk, kicked through the mess on the floor. He'd just had them last night. Where could they—and then he ripped open his guitar case and yelled, "Yes!" There were some of them—not all, but it would be enough. On his way downstairs he leafed through the stack. Hmm— a couple of the ones he had really wanted to do weren't here. But if they started with these, maybe...

"We're set," he said, pushing back into the garage. Jessica had passed cans of soda around to everybody, and Tyler grabbed a Dr Pepper. "Here—oh, shoot. Listen, I've only got one copy of each of these. Okay, here's what we do. I don't need one. We'll prop the one copy up here between you and Antonio, Wade. Pat, you weren't going to sing anyway, were you?"

Pat shook his head. "I'm okay."

Tyler saw Wade and Antonio glance at each other as they stepped closer together to share the one song sheet, and neither seemed happy. Well, he couldn't blame them; this practice hadn't gone very well so far. But he had some great songs here. If they could hold on till they heard this stuff . . .

"This first one's kind of funky; let's give it a little bit of a reggae feel—"

"All right!" Pat said, and launched into a laid-back, Bob Marley-sounding rhythm.

Antonio wrinkled his brow. "Whoa," he said. "I'm not really into reggae—"

"Just play it, man," Wade grumbled.

"Not the full Jamaica treatment or anything. Just a touch. Key of E," Tyler said. He strummed a couple of measures, trying his best to match his rhythm to the drums, but it was so different from the way he usually played it by himself that he had to concentrate.

He had just opened his mouth to start the vocal when Antonio said, "Hey, wait—what's wrong with your guitar?"

"Forget it, man," Wade said, still playing. "Keep going. It's close enough."

"No," Antonio said. "It's way off. I can't pick out a lead if the rhythm guitar's that far out of tune. In the mid-range—listen . . . jangle, jangle, jangle—you hear it?"

"I hear it," Wade said, "but let's—"

"No way." Antonio turned to Tyler. "How'd your guitar get out of tune so fast? How old are those strings?"

"Pretty old," Tyler admitted, shooting a sheepish glance at Jessica.

Antonio took off his Les Paul. "Let me try it."

Tyler handed over his guitar. Antonio strummed it. "How can you even play this thing? These strings are so old they're oxidized. I feel like—"

"What the . . ." a deep voice interrupted. "Did somebody turn this place into a lunatic asylum while I was gone?"

Everyone pivoted, following the voice. And as if things hadn't gone badly enough so far in this practice, here was Tyler's worst nightmare come true: his dad, home from his business trip a day early.

He stood by the garage's open side door. "Tyler, you want to explain this?"

"Uh—you're home early."

"Oh, hey, you noticed. But when I get here, I can't park in my own driveway, I don't recognize my own garage, and a bunch of refugees from Woodstock are making enough noise that I expect the cops any minute. What *is* this?"

Vacillating between panic and rage, Tyler fought for control. "We didn't expect you back till tomorrow."

"Obviously. Now . . ." And he gestured toward the musicians.

"It's a band practice, Dad. I was thinking about—"

"Who *are* these guys?"

Tyler glanced back at the guys; Pat looked a little freaked, but Wade and Antonio were glaring back at Tyler's dad, cold and hard. *Uh-oh.*

"Uh—the guy on the drums is Pat Johnson."

Pat waved a drumstick. "Pleased to—"

"I wasn't asking for a blasted introduction, Tyler!" his dad exploded. "I want to know why these misfits are in my garage with a bunch of expensive noisemakers, and all the stuff that usually sits— Tyler, you *idiot!*—you moved my *table saw? What were you thinking?*

Do you have any idea how hard it is to level that saw again?"

"I'll level the saw, Dad," Tyler said. "Just calm down. Please. This isn't a big deal. We'll put the garage back the way it was when we're done. I thought this was the best place to—"

"*When* you're done? You're done *now*. And I don't *want* you to level the saw, Tyler, because you'd just screw it up. Like anything else around here, if I want it done right, I have to do it myself. Your mom know about this?"

"I'm sorry, Mr. Jennings," Jessica said, stepping close to him. "This was my idea, really. I'm the one who asked the guys to come over."

Tyler's dad waved her off impatiently without looking at her. "Your mother know about this?" he repeated to Tyler.

A touchy question—Tyler didn't want to be the cause for another blowup between his parents. But he had to tell the truth. "Uh, yeah, we talked about it."

"But I notice she didn't stick around to listen to the noise."

Tyler heard a growl and turned. Wade and Antonio were putting their instruments back into their cases, but it was clear from Antonio's expression that he did *not* like hearing his guitar playing called noise. "Hey, no, guys," Tyler pleaded. "We'll get this worked out."

Wade shook his head. "Sounds like we better take off, man. Storm clouds movin' in."

"No, we can—"

"Didn't you hear me, Tyler?" his dad growled. "You guys are done here. Pack it up. Go play someplace else. This was a bad idea."

"Yeah, we'll go pollute somebody else's garage," Antonio muttered—quietly, but not quietly enough.

"*What?*" Tyler's dad hissed.

Antonio stopped what he was doing and looked up. There was no give in his eyes. A split second of stillness as everybody analyzed the situation—and then Tyler stepped between the two of them, faced his dad squarely, and said, "Listen—all right, Dad, this obviously wasn't such a great idea. Sorry. My fault. I'll help 'em pack up, we'll get the cars out of the driveway, and when you get ready to move the stuff in the garage, let me know and I'll help. Why don't you go on in the house, check the mail, and by the time—"

"Don't you patronize me, Tyler," his dad said. "That's about the stupidest thing you can do." He pointed at Antonio. "I want to know what this guy—"

Jessica stepped close to Tyler's dad then, so close he couldn't ignore her. His arm, pointing at Antonio, hung over her shoulder. Even though she was much shorter than he was, she stared right up into his eyes, and he looked down at her. "Mr. Jennings," she said in a low, slow voice, "I can't tell you how awful I feel about this. It really was all my idea. And now everyone's all upset, and it's my fault. Please—let Tyler and me help the guys get their stuff packed up so they can leave. We'll be quick. Please? So I don't have to feel worse than I already do?"

His dad scowled at her, then scowled at Tyler and Antonio, and stood sullenly for a minute. No one moved or spoke. Then he shifted slightly, and the tension was broken. "All right," he growled. "Tyler, you've pulled some boneheaded stunts in your life." He picked up his briefcase. "But you've set a new record for stupidity with this one. You *will* pay." He disappeared through the door into the kitchen.

Tyler rubbed his face. How he hated that man. He had wanted this so badly for so long, and now, here was his chance, and his dad had found a way to mess it up. "Listen, guys—I'm sorry, man. I thought the coast was clear till tomorrow."

Wade shrugged. "Hey, not your fault. Practice wasn't goin' that great anyway."

Tyler laughed uneasily. "Yeah, I know what you mean. But it was pickin' up at the end there, by the time we got the background vocals worked in and everything. Why don't we start over somewhere else? You guys have any place you usually practice?" He pressed the garage door opener.

"Hey!" Jessica said. "You guys could practice in *my* garage! Why didn't I think of that?"

Wade shook his head. "I don't think so, man." He toted his amplifier back over to the van, hoisted it in. "It wasn't happenin'. I didn't feel a band comin' together here. Music wasn't there."

Tyler carried a couple of the mikes and stands to the van. "But how can you tell so soon? We only had a few minutes—"

"Nah, he's right," Antonio said. "When you get a bunch of musicians together, and it doesn't click right away, no point in pushin' it—it ain't gonna happen."

Tyler stood, frozen and desperate—how could he keep this dream from slipping away? Things seemed to be happening in slow motion now—every word, every expression on the musicians' faces, was incredibly significant. He turned toward the drummer. "Pat?"

Pat was putting his drums back in their heavy cases. "Hey, a drummer and a rhythm guitarist do not a band make."

In only a few minutes, Wade's van was packed and he and Antonio were inside, with the engine running. Jessica leaned through Wade's open window, talking animatedly to him, but Tyler could see him shaking his head as he replied. Finally, Jessica stepped back, upset and disappointed, and Wade headed down the driveway, with one lazy wave of his hand back at Tyler.

Tyler helped Pat load the last of his drum cases into his little station wagon. "Well, that could have gone better," Pat said.

"Listen, Pat," Tyler said, grasping at his last chance. "What if I get a couple other guys to play bass and lead guitar. Or even keyboards. You still interested?"

Pat seemed uneasy. "I don't know," he said. "Really, Wade was right—it wasn't comin' together. And I got some other gigs, some other guys talkin' about a band . . ."

"It was startin' to click there at the end, though, didn't you think? If we could build on that . . ."

Pat looked away, shook his head, then closed the tailgate of the wagon. "Okay, Tyler, the thing is . . . I mean, I didn't really get to hear your songs or anything, but one thing that was real obvious when you were doin' those lead vocals . . . I mean, the truth is, you're just not—"

There was a soft sound behind Tyler, and he heard Jessica's voice from behind his shoulder. "Pat, I'm so sorry this happened. You were so sweet to come. You know, really, some other time . . ."

Pat smiled at her, then shrugged. "Who knows? Hey, you two take it easy." And he hopped into his car, waving out the open driver's window as he sped down the driveway.

Tyler stood watching Pat's car disappear down the street. He felt paralyzed. He knew he should move, talk to Jessica, talk to his dad, begin to clean the garage, something. But his body felt heavy, his head dark and empty.

Jessica stood beside him, her hand on his arm, her body pressed against him.

And he had no idea how long they stood that way before he became aware of something else—another voice. His dad, back in the garage now and muttering.

His dad. His dad who somehow managed to find some way to

mess up just about everything Tyler ever tried to do. His dad who made life miserable for everyone in his family. His dad who never thought of anyone but himself. His dad who *cared* for no one but himself. His dad who seemed to love to spend time away from home but who nevertheless had found some way to come home early and screw up the best thing that had happened to Tyler in a long, long time. And Tyler turned toward the garage and glared at his dad, who stood there, hands on hips, shaking his head and muttering. And Tyler felt his eyes narrowing, his jaw muscles clenching . . .

And then there was Jessica, staring up into his face. "Come on," she whispered, tugging on his arm. "We have to help your dad straighten up the garage. You promised. I'll talk to him, you straighten. Then let's go for a drive."

chapter 14

"Forget Wade and Antonio," Tyler said.

Jessica sighed, easing her Miata around the curves of Rock Canyon Road. Her headlights were on; the late afternoon sun didn't reach down into the narrow canyon. "But if I catch them in the right mood—"

"Jessica, they're not looking for the same kind of band I'm looking for. They're good, they're really good. But they're going to be happiest playing bars and dances, covering whatever kind of rock and pop songs the audience wants. That's what they've been doing, and that's what they want to keep on doing."

"So do it with them, Tyler! It'll be good experience. And maybe along the way—"

"That's not me."

"But as a start?"

Tyler shook his head slowly, eyes closed. "Not what I've been looking for."

The words burst out of her: "Oh, *Tyler*—you can be so *stubborn!* I went to a lot of trouble to set up this practice! And now it's all going to be wasted because you won't—"

"They play bars, Jessica. I'm underage! I couldn't even go in. Why would they want me in their band?"

"Well, if you talked with them, if you explained that . . . maybe they could . . ." Her voice trailed off.

After a moment, she took another approach. "What about Pat? He's never played with Wade and Antonio before anyway. Start with him, add a few other players . . ."

Tyler winced as he thought of Pat's last comment to him, interrupted when Jessica stepped up: *Okay, Tyler . . . one thing that was real obvious when you were doin' those lead vocals . . . I mean, the truth is, you're just not—*Tyler didn't have any problem imagining what Pat would have said:

Tyler, you're just not any good.

Tyler, you just don't have what it takes.

Tyler, every tone-deaf vocalist in every lousy garage band in the city sings better than you. Besides that, you're lousy on guitar, and I don't want to be in a band with you, not today, not tomorrow, not ever. Period. Have a nice life.

No, Pat was out.

They drove in silence. After a few minutes, Jessica said, "You're awfully quiet. What are you thinking?"

He shrugged. How could he even begin to explain? "Have you ever wanted something so badly for so long that you could just . . . just . . ." How could he put into words what he was feeling, the thick blackness that was enveloping him? He tried again. "For years, all I've wanted is to serve God, and to do it through music. I practice at least an hour a day. I work hard on the songs I write. I listen hard to my CDs, trying to figure out how the musicians are doing what they're doing, how they arrange their material, how the songwriters get the power they get out of just a few words."

He watched her. She looked toward him, urging him with her eyes to keep talking, but he could tell he hadn't connected yet. "I read my Bible, searching for the messages God wants me to communicate through my songs. I pray for an opportunity. And today, I watched my chance to put together a band to do all that—"

"But, Tyler, if the way you get to do your church music is by first playing at dances and parties and things, why is that wrong? Everybody has to start somewhere. What I say is, let's keep trying with Wade and Antonio, or if not with them then with Pat, and just get *some* kind of band together and play wherever you can. Play whatever kind of music people want to hear, Tyler!"

He looked at her, so near him in the small car. She glanced at him briefly, encouragingly, then cut her eyes back to the curving road. She was so beautiful. He allowed himself a second, as she drove, to let his eyes wander from the beauty of her face down to her slim shoulders and arms, the soft sweater that hugged her figure.

No, the truth was, Jessica probably *didn't* know what it was like to want something so badly and then lose her one chance to get it. She was breathtakingly, heartbreakingly beautiful, she was rich, she knew how to maneuver in the world—she got what she wanted, one way or another.

The words "Jessica" and "disappointment" didn't go together. Except maybe for those who fell in love with her.

He looked back at the road, then out the side window at the creek crashing among boulders beside them.

"And if not that, then there must be another way," she said, sounding a little impatient. "Other musicians. There are musicians at your church, right? Maybe some of them—"

"Jessica . . ." He rubbed his eyes. "I've tried. We talked about this before. I just, uh—right now I can't think about this."

She reached with her right hand and patted his knee. "Poor Tyler. I know. We'd both looked forward to this for so long, and then how frustrating to have your dad come home and ruin the whole thing."

A surge of anger ran through Tyler at the thought of his dad. And then he remembered Jessica stepping up to his dad at the end, when it looked like he and Antonio were going to get violent, and changing the whole mood. She had that power. Tyler wasn't sure how he felt about that. But today, it had come in handy.

She took his hand, squeezed it, held on. "I'm here for you, Tyler. I hope you know that."

He gripped her hand, glad for the comfort of her touch. But the truth was, she didn't know—*couldn't* know—the depth of his disappointment, or the desperate power of his desire to sing and to serve God through his music.

He remembered Becca's words about Jessica from earlier that day: *One of the things I talked about was my faith, about how important God is to me . . . It wasn't like she was rejecting it—it was like she didn't get it. Tyler, this is not a girl who has a spiritual dimension to her. At least not yet.*

Jacie had said it: *She just lives in a different world from you.*

Jessica's gentle touch helped. And her genuine desire to "be there" for him.

But right now he needed more.

● ● ●

He hopped into his Escort when Jessica dropped him off. She had someplace to go, she said, and it wasn't until after she'd rushed off down the street in her red Miata that it occurred to Tyler to wonder whether that meant a date—and, in fact, whether that date wasn't with Wade. Had that been part of the deal that had resulted in this band practice, part of what they'd been talking about through Wade's van window?

Tyler was too deep in despair to care. He drove aimlessly downtown, stopped briefly in the parking lot of the convenience store, and eyed the payphone, thinking of calling Allen collect—he really needed Allen badly right now—but knew that Allen was too broke to pay for collect calls. He pulled back out onto the street and wandered through the neighborhoods, passed Richard's house and thought about dropping in, but somehow Richard didn't seem like what Tyler needed just now.

He didn't really decide to go to Jacie's house; his car just went there on its own, and Tyler found himself parked at the curb in front. Should he go in? She might not even be home. And even if she were, would it be fair to her to dump all this on her, to ruin her day because his was such a bust?

But then somehow he was outside his car, walking across the brown, dormant grass, and then knocking on her front door. Jacie answered it, grinned widely in wonderful surprise, said "Ty—" And then her face shifted as she studied him. She froze, compassion and concern filling that honest face that could never hide what she was feeling, and then she pulled him inside. "Just a minute," she said.

He stood by the door as she rushed into the kitchen. He heard her make two phone calls. Short ones. Each consisted of only one word before she hung up: "Alyeria."

chapter 15

Tyler sat breaking sticks into tiny pieces, flicking each scrap away, watching them sail into the bushes in the twilight. Jacie sat close to him on his left, Solana on his right, their shoulders snuggled against his, and Becca leaned against him from behind. On a normal day, this would have been more affectionate contact than Tyler would have been able to stand from his friends for more than a few minutes. But this was no normal day.

He reached down and grabbed a couple more sticks from the ground.

They'd been sitting in Alyeria for 10 minutes or so already, all of them bundled in coats and gloves on this cold December evening with the threat of snow in the air, and no one had said a thing. Tyler almost thought it would be better to say nothing, but that was stupid—why had he been drawn to Jacie's house if not to talk to his closest friends about what had happened?

Still, he opened his mouth three times to speak before he actually formed the first words. "It was pretty much of a bust," he said finally. Then he lapsed into silence again. Jacie leaned closer. Tyler broke off a few more pieces, flicked them away. Comforted by the presence of his friends, he narrowed his attention to the task of trying to get one of the twigs he flicked to land in a woodpecker hole in one of the trees around him, shutting out his despair, and almost forgot to say anything until Solana stirred, changing her position. Then the blackness crept back, and he sighed. "Wade and Antonio were good. Really good. Pat Johnson—from school? You know him?"

"I had math with him one year," Becca said.

"He was the drummer. He was okay—not as experienced as Wade and Antonio. Anyway..." Tyler closed his eyes, rubbed his face with his glove, chuckled sadly. "I can't imagine what else could have gone wrong. I mean, first of all, I looked like a complete dork. Antonio had a Les Paul, and I had my crummy guitar with old strings and no amp. Once I finally got in tune, I couldn't catch on to the beat. And when we finally got around to trying some of my songs, all I had was one lousy copy of the words. They wanted lead sheets, whatever that is. And just when I thought things might be looking up, guess what? My dad came home."

Jacie looked up sharply. "Your *dad?* I thought—"

"Yeah, well, so did I, but he got home early. And he was not pleased."

Tyler flicked a few more pieces of twig. Jacie reached over and touched his arm gently for a moment. No words, just that touch. He knew he didn't have to describe the whole ugly scene with his dad. These three would know. And understand.

Even though he wasn't describing it, he found himself reliving that scene—going back over, in his mind, every expression on his dad's face, every harsh word, every rush of desperation and humiliation Tyler had felt during those tense moments.

"You know what?" he found himself saying. "I don't love my dad. I should. But the truth is, I don't. I'm afraid of him. Sometimes I hate him. But I never—"

"Tyler," Jacie interrupted, sounding confused and a little frightened. "You don't hate your dad. I mean—he's your *dad*. Whatever he's done, he's—"

"Jacie, Jacie," Solana scolded mildly, as if she were speaking to a child. "Do you really think Tyler needs you to give him a guilt trip about this? Why should he love his dad—would you love that man if he were your dad?"

Jacie looked confused and opened her mouth to speak again. But she stopped, then looked back at Tyler, urging him with her eyes to go on.

"The thing is," Tyler continued, "it's not just me. Week after week, I have to watch him hurting my mom. And Tyra. I've watched her go up to her room and lie on her bed and cry for hours after he's raked her over the coals. He's just—the man is cruel. He is a mean guy. Period. And I don't really care why—I'm not interested in his fears or anxieties or frustrations or what happened in his childhood. Who cares? I just want him to go away. So there. Now you know."

A Steller's jay landed in the tree Tyler had been trying to hit with the twigs, cocked its blue-black head at him, pumped its top-knot a couple of times, and squawked. Tyler sensed the girls raising their heads to look at it too, then leaning back into him when the jay flew away, quickly disappearing into the darkness. Tyler hadn't realized how late it was getting.

"So do you think I'm horrible?" he asked after a pause.

By way of answer, all three of the girls, as if on cue, lifted a hand and gently, lovingly touched him—on the arm, on the shoulder, on the knee. Again, no words. Just that touch.

Their touch was different from Jessica's, Tyler realized. Their touch gave. They were offering something to him—understanding, sympathy, strength—something of themselves. Even through the layers of clothes, he could almost feel the warm blood flowing from them into him through their touch. Jessica's touch—well, she offered something too, as well as she could, but it was also a way of claiming him—of indicating that he was hers. A grasping rather than a giving. Like writing her name on him by leaving a handprint. As if her touch were pulling something out of him into her.

Jacie shifted; they'd been sitting in the cold for a long time. The girls were probably getting uncomfortable. But they continued to sit, snuggling close to him, supporting him, even if they were uncomfortable. He was lucky, he realized in a rush of feeling, to have such friends.

"Well," he said, "I guess I'll never have a band now."

A brief pause as the girls thought that over, then Becca said, "Well, never say never. You know, Tyler—God didn't give you your love of music for no reason. It fits somehow. But maybe not in a band, not right now."

"And anyway," Solana said, leaning close and looking up, batting her eyelashes, "you've still got us."

Tyler chuckled. "Yeah. I do." Then he laughed. "Speaking of which . . . I mean, think about it. When Jessica came back to town, what we were all talking about—arguing about, really—was which of the two new girls in my life would make the best girlfriend. Here I sit two weeks later, and I don't have either of them." He stood, and the girls slowly, stiffly got to their feet around him. "Hannah's unattainable—I mean, you can't get to her without her dad's permission, and he probably thinks I'm a pervert."

"Smart man," Solana said.

"And Jessica—" He thought of his ride with Jessica after the band practice fell apart, of her attempts at helping him feel better, of his enjoyment of her physical beauty but of the lack of connection, of closeness, nevertheless. And how that connection had been so immediately established with Jacie, Solana, and Becca as soon as they flocked around him in his need. "Well, Jessica is Jessica. She's really not a bad girl, you know? She means well. I—well, I guess I finally hear what you've been telling me about Jessica."

The girls looked up at him, and there were no I-told-you-so's.

He held out his arms. "So you're still my three best friends." And the girls stepped into his hug. Once again, he slowly, deliberately kissed the top of each head.

"Careful kissing Becca," Solana warned, her voice muffled against his shoulder. "Probably get head lice."

"I'm not kissing," Tyler said. "Did you think I was kissing you guys? Yuck. I'm actually picking out the lice with my teeth."

"Well then stop it," Solana said. "I'm very particular about which guys I let pick my head lice out with their teeth. I'm not that easy."

"Despite your reputation," Jacie added, and Solana elbowed her.

They broke the hug slowly, but Solana and Jacie linked arms with him on either side, and Becca took Solana's other arm.

"Well, this is real nice and sweet and everything," Tyler said, "but I have no idea how we're going to get out of here linked up like this."

"We don't stop, we don't stop," Becca chanted, marching in place.

"Uh, I think those trees will stop you sure enough," Solana said.

"We go like crabs, sideways," Jacie said, leading the way through the narrow opening in the bushes.

As soon as they came out in the open on the other side, Tyler began trying to think of what this reminded him of, the four of them linked together arm in arm like this—some game they used to play. And then Becca shouted, "Hey! Let's do the Wizard of Oz thing! We haven't done that in years!"

Yep, that was it, Tyler thought. *Drat.* "You know, it's just remotely possible somebody might see us," he said.

"When did you start caring about that?" Solana snorted. "That's the beginning of the end, man. You're becoming an adult. First you don't want anybody to see you doing anything goofy, and the next thing you know, you stop picking your nose in public."

"No worries there; he'll never stop that," Becca said. "Besides, nobody'll see us—it's too dark! Come on!" She took a hop, then began striding ahead, singing,

> *"We're off to see the wizard!*
> *The wonderful Wizard of Oz!*
> *He really is a whiz of a wiz—"*

"I'm not doing this," Tyler said.

"You have to!" Solana shouted, finding Becca's stride and pulling the others along. "We need a tin man, and if ever anybody needed a heart, it's you!"

"Oh, yeah?" Tyler said. "Well, I guess that makes you the scarecrow, because you definitely need a brain."

"Well, I'm not Dorothy!" Becca laughed. There was a short pause. Then Tyler, Solana, and Becca yelled in unison, "Jacie!"

"Again?" Jacie said. "I *always* have to be Dorothy!"

"It's either that or Toto!" Solana laughed.

"Not this time," Tyler said, "because there isn't going to *be* a this time—count me out of the whole Wizard-walk thing." But the girls ignored him and immediately launched, with wide, swinging steps, into,

> *"We're off to see the wizard!*
> *The wonderful Wizard . . ."*

"Stop dragging me!" Tyler shouted.

"Wizard-walk or be tripped!" Solana shouted.

> *"If ever oh ever a whiz there was,*
> *The Wizard of Oz is one because,*
> *because, because, because, because, beCAUSE . . ."*

"You call that singing?" Tyler said.

"Yes!" Jacie shouted. "That's it! I just had a brainstorm!"

"I thought I heard thunder rumbling around in vast empty spaces," Tyler mumbled.

"We'll be your band, Tyler! We'll be your backup singers! We're good! Listen!"

> *"We're off the see the WiZARD . . ."*

"Yes," Tyler said, "we have a bright future ahead of us. I can see that right now. We can perform at funerals, construction sites, building demolitions, war zones—*oof!*"

Tyler hit the turf—but somehow neglected to let go of the arms on either side of him, and the four of them ended up in a squirming, laughing pile.

"You lefted when you should have righted!" Solana gasped, then burst into laughter again.

"I wasn't lefting or righting, either one—I was straight-aheading," Tyler protested when he could catch his breath.

"Tyler straight-aheading?" Becca squealed. "Not likely. His straight-aheader's been broke for years. He mostly lefts."

"That's not true. I . . . I . . ." And that was as much as he could get out. With all three girls poking and tickling him, Tyler gave up on words and concentrated on self-defense—which was futile, of course, against the three of them. And he pressed his head back into the grass and yelled with laughter, aware in some dim, still-rational corner of his mind that he hadn't enjoyed anything so much in a long time.

● ● ●

AllenOlson: So you don't even want to TALK about what happened at your band practice?

ColoradoTy: oh, we can talk about it. but let's save the details for some other day. short version: abc should have sent a crew down to film an episode of law and order during our practice. would have been a doozy. win an emmy for sure.

AllenOlson: That good, huh? So I conclude that there won't be any more practices with that particular group of guys, correct?

ColoradoTy: correctamundo.

AllenOlson: And how are you feeling about all this?

ColoradoTy: pretty lousy, to tell you the truth. at first i thought it was the end of the world. now i realize it was just the end of life as we know it. so things are lookin up. really, i think the issues with my dad, who came home and busted the whole thing up—or maybe i should say put it out of its misery—are worse than the band debacle. had a talk with J, S, and B about the whole deal and we ended up laughin, so a return to sanity is probably just around the corner. actually, even thought about givin you a call, but would have had to call collect at a million bucks a minute.

AllenOlson: Tell you what. I'm writing this down right now to remind myself. I'm going to send you a phone card—at only a hundred grand a minute—so next time something comes up and you want to chat over a wire instead of in cyberspace (whatever happened to the real world?), you can. But I'm glad to hear you were able to get with your gal friends.

ColoradoTy: yeah, they were definitely what the doctor ordered. hey, speaking of women, i have a confession.

AllenOlson: I will hear your confession now, my son. Speak freely, remembering that anything you say can and will be used against you in a court of law.

ColoradoTy: you know that thing you wanted me to do about jessica and hannah, projecting myself ten years into the future, imagining myself married to them, all that?

AllenOlson: I remember it well. What did you discover?

ColoradoTy: nothin, because i didn't do it. that's the confession. i mean, i tried, but shoot, how do i know what it would be like to be married to anybody? when i think of being married, i don't think of you and kathy or anybody good like that—i think of my parents, and who wants a marriage like that?

AllenOlson: Don't sell your parents' marriage short. For one thing, it's already lasted longer than the average, and that's something to celebrate in itself. And who knows what they'll be like in ten years? Yeah, I know your dad has his problems, but your mom is a remarkable woman; she makes up for a lot.

ColoradoTy: no argument there. but what i was tryin to say was, i had a pretty hard time imagining marriage, but i learned a few things about jessica and hannah anyway, just keepin my eyes open and thinkin about things.

AllenOlson: Such as?

ColoradoTy: oh, a lot of stuff. but lyin in bed last night, thinkin over the day—the lousy band practice, talkin with jessica, spendin good time with my brio squad—i came up with something i thought was pretty cool, and when i told my mom about it this morning on the way to church, she got all misty-eyed and everything. tyra told me to stop playin shrink.

AllenOlson: And what was this remarkable, misty-eyed revelation?

ColoradoTy: hannah and jessica are both at a fork in the road. nobody knows yet which road they'll take. well, god knows. but i don't, which is maybe one reason i couldn't do the ten-year thing.

AllenOlson: And what choice do our two young lovelies have to make?

ColoradoTy: different choice for each. jessica could go one way and be a really self-centered, shallow person who only cares about money, stuff, and gettin her own way, no matter who she hurts. controlling people to get what she wants. someone who talks but doesn't listen. or she could go the other way and be a compassionate, loving person who cares more about people than stuff. someone who uses stuff to help people.

but right now, see, she's right in the middle.

AllenOlson: I'm getting all misty-eyed myself. And Hannah?

ColoradoTy: hannah might get so caught up in rules and laws and lists of do's and don'ts that she becomes a pharisee. remember when you talked about modern pharisees?

AllenOlson: The fact that YOU remember moves me more than I can say. Yes, I remember.

ColoradoTy: well, hannah's right there. so sure she's right about everything. she could lose sight of god's love and forgiveness.

AllenOlson: And His grace.

ColoradoTy: yeah, the whole grace thing. she could end up majoring in wrath and judgment. so if that's the road she takes, she'll be a finger-pointer, self-righteous, sayin ``thank god i'm not like the rest of those sinners.'' or, of course, she could take the other road and become an example of god's love and mercy to everybody around her. loving, compassionate, someone who smiles rather than frowns, who accepts and loves people as they are, just like jesus did.

AllenOlson: I'm nearly speechless, my man, but I have just enough voice left to ask: What does this revelation mean for your future relationships with these two fine young ladies?

ColoradoTy: oh, i'll date jessica still, but we'll both date other people. it won't be like last year. she's still a heck of a woman, allen. she has qualities and strengths the brio squad still hasn't noticed. besides, she's hot. want to hear a funny thing?

AllenOlson: Shoot.

ColoradoTy: when guys see a beautiful girl, they look right past her bad qualities, even the obvious ones, and think she's great. when other girls see a beautiful girl, they look right past her good qualities, even the obvious ones, and think she's ms. satan herself.

AllenOlson: LOL. Okay, wipe my eyes, and I ask: What about Hannah?

ColoradoTy: what about her? the door's locked and deadbolted, man. the sign is posted: thou shalt not date on pain of being toasted by the fire-breathing daddy. so i remain interested, and i'll see her when i can at school and stuff. i mean, what else can i do?

AllenOlson: So the next chapter will read: Tyler Bides His Time. Yes, a good approach on both fronts. The guru is proud of you, Tyler. He really is. And now the guru must rush off or he will be late for his Bible study small group, which he is supposed to lead, so late is definitely bad. The guru thanks you, kind lad, for your gifts of rice and beads, and for trudging so faithfully up the mountain barefoot through the snow just for my wise counsel. May it serve you well. And may the eternal light always shine in your heart, dear one.

ColoradoTy: yeah, you too, fat old wrinkled guy. may your rice bowl always be full, and may you not embarrass your kids too much. may the force be with you. may kathy continue to be blind to your abundant faults. etc. etc.

AllenOlson: Greet the sistren with a holy kiss for me. Love to all. Bye for now.

Epilogue

"Why didn't we decide to shoot this inside on a sound stage or something?" Jack said, and everyone laughed.

It was another *Brio* photo shoot, a week after the ill-fated band practice and three weeks after the photo shoot at which Jessica had unexpectedly shown up. Tyler, stepping into the toe bindings of his Rossignol cross-country skis, new for Christmas last year, was well aware of how ironic it was that they were all here again, reassembled like some class reunion or something, but this time on a sunny, snow-covered slope above the hot springs resort for skiing photos.

"Come on, Jack, you wuss!" Richard said. "Believe me, this is not cold for skiing. In fact, the snow's soft and sloppy. It would be better if it was about 15 degrees colder." In the bright, Colorado-blue noon sky, there were occasional clouds off toward the horizon, but the sun blazed down unobstructed from overhead.

"Yeah, well, my fingers are freezing," Jack answered. "You get to wear gloves. I have to keep taking mine off to adjust my cameras.

Plus—you guys get to wear sunglasses, while I have to let the glare from the snow destroy my vision."

"Yes, Jack," Tyler's mom said, "you deserve combat pay. Such a tough life photographers lead, photographing beautiful girls on a lovely day in Colorado . . ."

Earlier that week, Tyler had asked his mom, "Are you *sure* you want Jessica at the photo shoot?"

"She's perfect," his mom had said. "I'm choosing models, remember, not a future daughter-in-law, and she'll be stylish, cute—I think she completes the group very nicely for this shoot. Don't look at me that way! I'm not being inconsistent."

"No, of course not. I would never accuse you of that. Far be it from me to ever suggest—"

"Don't overdo it."

"Well, the last time you didn't want her in the shoot. And you've never been crazy about me dating her."

His mom leaned closer and looked right into his eyes. "This will surprise you then, but I *do* like Jessica, and I worry about her, too. I thought your realization about Jessica the other day was dead-on, about the decisions she has to make about what kind of person she wants to be. And I worry very much that she'll make the wrong choice. Maybe, Tyler, just maybe, giving her a chance to hang around with the Brio crowd will help her make the right choices."

"In that case maybe I'd better schedule her for some heavy evangelistic dating this winter on Friday and Saturday nights," Tyler said, wiggling his eyebrows.

His mom laughed. "Vast experience with girls like Jessica tells me they learn positive lessons better from other girls than from guys, Tyler."

"Whoa! Tyler! You with us?" Jack's voice asked, and Tyler shook off the memory.

"Wake up, Tyler!" Becca yelled.

"No, I'm here," he said. "I'm fine. Point me where you want me to go."

"Alicia, please direct our daydreaming friend on where to stand, and then hasten back to the lodge and get me about 10 gallons of hot coffee, an Arctic parka, and a propane space heater, would you please?"

The first significant snowfall of the year—at least down at the town's elevation—had come this past week, about eight inches of fresh powder. Not a minute too soon for Jack, because he was already behind schedule getting some photos for a skiing layout in *Brio*. Not a minute too soon for Tyler, either—he had found himself ready to hang up his mountain bike and climbing gear for the year and dust off the skis.

Alicia put Tyler in a close twosome with Jessica, whose bright, stretch ski outfit would have looked more at home on the downhill slopes. "All right, just chat," Jack called. "Look happy."

"I'll try," Jessica said, smiling at Tyler, "but every time I get on cross-country skis, I wonder—what's the point? It's so much more fun to ride a ski lift up a mountain and swoosh down than to put these things on and walk around."

Tyler wore no hat, and a cold breeze stirred his hair. "I won't argue with that," Tyler said. "I'm a downhill fanatic. But on these, I could take you places this winter you can't get to any other way, and show you things that nobody else will see. And I love racing on these things. It's a whole different sport."

"That it is," she agreed. "And the answer is yes."

"It is?"

"Yeah. To taking me places this winter on cross-country skis."

Tyler couldn't help it; he quickly scanned the hillside to see where the other four girls were. They were 30 yards away, huddled around a thermos of hot chocolate, giggling. Hannah, who insisted that she couldn't ski, was the only one not wearing skis. She wore fat snow boots she'd borrowed from Becca. "Sounds good," he said. He remembered Becca's attempts to witness to Jessica, and resolved to make their cross-country ski date a foursome with Becca and Nate.

"All right," Jack said, stepping down from the small ladder he'd dragged all the way out there. What was it with this guy and ladders? "Now I need all the ladies—Jacie! Becca! Could you bring the rest of your crew over here please? Tyler, you and Richard go find Bigfoot or something."

Tyler heard the swoosh of skis behind him, and then Richard slapped a hand on his shoulder. "Got one!" he called.

"Hey!" Tyler yelled, holding up one ski to show off his size 11 boots. "You call this big? You ought to take a look at Nate's 13s!"

"Watch what you say about Nate," Becca smiled as she skied up, followed closely by Jacie, Solana, and Hannah. "Just because he has big feet doesn't mean—"

"Tyler! Richard!" Jack yelled. "Vamoose! I need to get these ladies into their places. Alicia, what's next?"

Richard and Tyler skate-skied to the thermos and poured some hot chocolate into Styrofoam cups. "I don't know how you do it, my friend," Richard said, sipping the steaming hot drink.

"Do what?"

"Think back three weeks. I'd have said after that last photo shoot that within a month at least half of the beautiful maidens you see over there taking directions from a frozen photographer wouldn't be speaking to you. You'd have chosen either Jessica or Hannah, and either way the other four would be ticked. Well, maybe not Jacie. She seems to put up with you even at your most annoying. But as near as I can tell they're *all* still your friends. You've got the magic touch."

Tyler shook his head, watching the girls clowning for Jack's camera. "No magic touch, and no secret. Actually, I pretty much made the same mistake J.P. did."

Richard almost spit out his hot chocolate. "You did *what?* With who?"

Tyler laughed. "Not that mistake. I meant that I somehow got egotistical enough to think that the only thing that mattered here was which girl I wanted to date, and that when I made up my mind, they would all automatically go along with it."

"Yeah, I remember J.P. saying something like that."

"Well, surprise, surprise. Hannah wasn't about to change her commitment to courtship so she could date me. And when I sat down with Jessica this week to carefully explain that even though she and I could date, I wasn't looking for anything exclusive, she burst out laughing."

"She *what?*" Richard laughed.

"Hey, don't bust a gut. She recovered pretty quickly so she wouldn't hurt my feelings, and then she said that she hoped she hadn't given me the impression she was looking for something exclusive herself. She kissed me on the cheek, called me sweet, and said that she hadn't been back in town long enough to tie herself to just one person." Tyler almost blushed, remembering the moment, and his embarrassment at her response. "I felt, as you can imagine, pretty stupid. Will you stop laughing, please?"

Richard had spilled most of his hot chocolate onto the snow. "I can't help it!" he choked out. "All that agonizing over which girl! All that tension with your Brio chicks!"

"Keep it down over there!" Jack called. "I'm trying to concentrate!"

"Yeah," Tyler said. "Well, I may be an idiot in many ways, but I'm smart enough to realize why you think this is so funny. You're figuring maybe you can date Jessica yourself."

"Oh, don't be cruel," Richard chuckled. "She'd never go out with me in a million years."

"Richard," Tyler said with a smile, "stranger things have happened."

"Nothing stranger than that has *ever* happened," Richard argued. "I can't conceive of any possible way Jessica and I will ever come into close personal contact unless I ram her new Miata with my—"

"Now I need one guy and all the skiing girls!" Jack called. "Richard! Hustle! Hannah, skiers only in this one. Take five."

Tyler poured another cup of hot chocolate as Hannah plodded up toward him and Richard joined the group for the photo. "Need to warm up?" he smiled, handing her the steaming cup.

"Oh, yes, thanks, Tyler." She sipped the chocolate, looking over the rim at him.

Even though she had undoubtedly never bought so much as a pair of socks at Cadwallader & Finch, Tyler thought she was still about the most beautiful thing he'd ever seen. Even in the cheap hat she'd probably got at Kmart. Her face was so beautiful, who would notice the hat? He nodded toward her boots. "You know—it's not that hard to learn to ski. And you wouldn't believe how much fun—"

She silenced him with an upheld hand and licked chocolate off her lips—something Tyler could have watched her do all day long. "Tried it," she said. "And I don't even want to tell you how bad I was. Believe me, we're all safer if I stay off skis."

"Was that in Michigan?"

She nodded and took another sip. Steam rose around her face.

"Well, then, obviously you didn't have the benefit of a teacher like me," Tyler said. "I could have you gliding like a pro in two or three hours, guaranteed."

She giggled. "Or my money back?"

"Yup." He waited, but she didn't say anything more. "Hey, I'm serious," he said. "And we can get Jacie and the rest to come along, so even the most suspicious minds would have to admit it isn't a date."

She laughed. "That's sweet."

"So is it a date, then?" he asked. And when her eyes shot open, he laughed. "Just teasing!"

She scolded him playfully with her eyes, then said, "Maybe. We'll see."

"Okay, the whole cast now!" Jack yelled. "Everybody! Before my fingers freeze off!"

Tyler took Hannah's cup and threw both empties into the trash bag. He and Hannah headed down the gentle incline toward the group.

"Jack," Richard said, "it's almost 40 degrees out today. Fingers freezing off seems like a scientific impossibility. Personally, I'm too hot."

"Too hot? You talking about temperature or sex appeal?" Becca asked, causing Richard to blush.

"I'm," Solana rapped, "too hot for my hat ... too hot for my car ..."

"Thank you, Solana, for the sound track for this final shot," Jack said. "Last shot today, and it'll be the last shot of the magazine spread, too—a close-up of all your smiling faces crowded together, just happy smiles and eyes, okay? Lots of togetherness after a long day of skiing, bosom buddies, having so much fun you can hardly stand it, all that.

Tyler, I want you down here front and center. Down on one knee and crouch a little so everybody else can squeeze around you. That's right. Okay, the rest of you take your skis off so you can get cozy. Jacie and Solana, crowd in on either side. Good and close, because I want you both cheek-to-cheek with him."

Jacie put her cheek next to his, then turned her head and whispered, her lips brushing his ear, her breath hot on his cheek: "Alyeria. Always Alyeria, my wonderful friend," so softly that he knew even Solana, just inches away, couldn't hear it.

"Becca," Jack said, "get right behind him so you can put your chin on top of his head."

"Do I get to put my boot on his rear end, too?" she asked, settling in.

"Later," Jack said. "We'll take turns. But for now, I want the other three of you positioned around these four. Alicia, you want to help here? Richard, position yourself just to Becca's left—that's it. Hannah, to Becca's right—closer, everybody, closer! I don't want any space between you. Jessica, throw your arm around Richard's shoulders—yes, perfect—and your cheek right up to his. Yes, very—Tyler, will you stop laughing, please! You're about to cause the whole thing to come tumbling down, and then—"

"How can I put my chin on your head if your head is bouncing around?" Becca said. "Stop it! Right now!"

"Okay," Tyler squeaked. "I think I've got it under control. I think—" And then he lost it completely when he felt Becca's hands slide around his rib cage and begin tickling. Jacie and Solana leaned heavily in on him on either side, as if they were trying to push him over in two directions at once.

"Shoot it, Jack!" Tyler heard his mom yell. "Just like that! Quick!"

Two seconds later, the pile fell over and Tyler, his face buried in cold, grainy snow, snow down the back of his neck, couldn't tell who he was tickling and wrestling and who was tickling him.

"Did you get it?" Tyler's mom called.

"I think so," Jack said. "I got two shots off."

Tyler poked his head out of the pile long enough to ask, "Do we have to do it again? I don't think I'd survive."

"You guys couldn't do that again if you tried!" his mom laughed. "But if it turns out—that's a cover. Definitely a cover."

And as he was pulled back into the fray, the last thing Tyler heard was Richard screaming, "Let's try it again! Try it again!"

FIND A FRIEND!

THE CHRISTY MILLER SERIES

Beginning with 14-year-old Christy Miller's commitment to Christ, this bestselling series follows her high school years as she grows in her faith. But as for every real-life teen, things are not always easy. She shares the same hopes, worries, and joys, and has to make the same tough choices that you do every day.

Author Robin Jones Gunn fills the books with stories on friendship, dating, responsibility, life at school, and sticking up for what's right—all the things that are most important to teens like you. Her beloved character Christy Miller has become a friend for over a million teens around the world and is ready to meet you today!

1. Summer Promise
2. A Whisper and a Wish
3. Yours Forever
4. Surprise Endings
5. Island Dreamer
6. A Heart Full of Hope
7. True Friends
8. Starry Night
9. Seventeen Wishes
10. A Time to Cherish
11. Sweet Dreams
12. A Promise Is Forever

✦ BETHANYHOUSE

11400 Hampshire Ave. S. • Minneapolis, MN 55438 • 800-328-6109 • www.bethanyhouse.com

Become a Brio Girl Yourself!

You've made it to the end of this book. But that doesn't mean the great reading is over! Check out Focus on the Family's *Brio* magazine. Written for teens like you, each month's issue is packed with quality reading on tons of cool stuff! Articles and columns dig into fiction, faith, fashion and food ... and of course—guys! And it's all from a Christian perspective. Don't miss your chance to belong to an awesome group of *Brio* readers. Everyone's so close, they're like sisters.

Request a complimentary copy of this hot read *today* and become a *Brio* sis!

CALL   Focus on the Family at 1-800-A-FAMILY (in Canada, call 1-800-661-9800)

LOG ON   to www.briomag.org

OR WRITE   to Focus on the Family, Colorado Springs, CO 80995 (in Canada, write P.O. Box 9800, Stn. Terminal, Vancouver, B.C. V6B 4G3)

Mention that you saw this offer in the back of this book.

For more information about Focus on the Family and what branches exist in various countries, dial up our Web site at www.family.org.

Check Out Focus on the Family's

The Christy Miller Series

Teens across the country adore Christy Miller! She has a passion for life, but goes through a ton of heart-wrenching circumstances. Though the series takes you to a fictional world, it gives you plenty of "food for thought" on how to handle tough issues as they come up in your

The Nikki Sheridan Series

An adventurous spirit leads Nikki Sheridan, an attractive high school junior, into events and situations that will sweep you into her world and leave you begging for the next book in this captivating, six-book set!

Sierra Jensen Series

The best-selling author of The Christy Miller Series leads you through the adventures of Sierra Jensen as she faces the same issues that you do as a teen today. You'll devour every exciting story, and she'll inspire you to examine your own life and make a deeper commitment to Christ!

Mind Over Media: The Power of Making Sound Entertainment Choices

You can't escape the ideas and images that come from the media, but you *can* weed through the bad and grasp the good! This video uses an exciting, MTV-style production to dissolve the misconceptions people have about the media. The companion book uses humor, questions, facts and stories to help you take charge of what enters your mind and then directs your actions.

Life on the Edge—Live!

This award-winning national radio call-in show gives teens like you something positive to tune in to every Saturday night. You'll get a chance to talk about the hottest issues of your generation—no topic is off-limits! See if it airs in your area by visiting us on the Web at www.lifeontheedgelive.com.

Cool Stuff on Hot Topics!

My Truth, Your Truth, Whose Truth?

Who's to say what's right and wrong? This book shatters the myth that everything is relative and shows you the truth about absolute truth! It *does* matter . . . and is found only in Christ! Understand more about this hot topic in the unique video *My Truth, Your Truth, Whose Truth?*

No Apologies: The Truth About Life, Love and Sex

Read the truth about sex—the side of the story Hollywood doesn't want you to hear—in this incredible paperback featuring teens who've made decisions about premarital sex. You'll learn you're worth the wait. Discover more benefits of abstinence in the video *No Apologies: The Truth About Life, Love and Sex.*

Masquerade

In this hard-hitting, 30-minute video, popular youth speaker Milton Creagh uses unrehearsed footage of hurting teens to "blow the cover" off any illusions that even casual drug use is OK.

The Ultimate Baby-sitter's Survival Guide

Want to become everyone's favorite baby-sitter? This book is packed with practical information. It also features an entire section of safe, creative and downright crazy indoor and outdoor activities that will keep kids challenged, entertained and away from the television.

Dare 2 Dig Deeper Girl's Package

Have you been looking for info on the issues you deal with? Yeah, that's what we thought. So we put some together for you from our popular Dare 2 Dig Deeper booklets with topics  that are for girls only, such as: friendship, sexual abuse, eating disorders and purity. Set includes: *Beyond Appearances, A Crime of Force, Fantasy World, Forever, Friends, Hold On to Your Heart* and *What's the Alternative?*

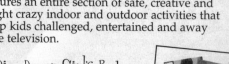

Visit us on the Web at
www.family.org or www.fotf.ca in Canada.

DATE DUE

The Library Store   #47-0103